All Women are Stupid Sometimes

Published by Asta Publications
P.O. Box 1735
Stockbridge, Georgia
For ordering info visit www.astapublications.com
For author info visit www.imanisbookshelf.com

Publisher's note
This is a work of fiction. All events and characteristics in this story are solely
the product of the author's imagination. Any similarities between any charac-
ters and situations presented in this book to any individuals, living or dead,
or actual places and situations are purely coincidental.

This book has been professional edited by Sue McKinney

Graphics by Keon Green of KTG WORKS for more info visit: www.ktgworks.
com

Text and composition: Kim Nakiya Howard-Carswell

Library of Congress Cataloging in Publication Data
Bell, Shelly
  All Women are Stupid Sometimes: a novel / Shelly Bell
    p. cm.

Includes index
        ISBN: 0-9777060-4-4
        ISBN: 13 978-0-9777060-4-4
        LCCN: 2007929513

First Asta Publications, LLC trade paperback edition July 2007
1. African American women-Fiction. 2. African American relationships-Fiction.
3. Self-realization-Fiction. 4.Drama-Ficition. 5. Urban-Fiction. I. Title

Printed and bound in the United States of America.

All Women are Stupid Sometimes

By Shelly Bell

ASTA PUBLICATIONS

This Book is dedicated to my children Imani and Josiah, to my mother Stephanie, my dad Genavous Sr. and my brother Genavous Jr.

A special thank you to my Aunt Wilhelmina (Smoochie), Aunt Chandra (Boo Boo), Grandma Wilhelmina, Grandma Helen, Uncle Kevin and all of my family and friends who kept me encouraged through my learning experiences.

Rest In Peace My Guardian Angel
Beverly T. Caldwell

I BELIEVE IN THE IMPOSSIBLE

Impossibility is made up only in your mind, if you think you can, **You Will**, if you think you can't, **You Won't**………we always claim to be waiting on the Lord, imagine what you could have if you could only realize that he is waiting on **YOU**!

All Women are Stupid Sometimes

PROLOGUE

"Are you fucking him?!"

I almost spit my drink in her face when I blurt out, "Excuse me?"

"Are you fucking him?!" Trinity shouts when at this point all she knows about me is the fact that I just finished hugging her ex-boyfriend, Mitchell, who she is obsessed with.

"Think fast, Celeste," I tell myself. Knowing that I am not fucking him, but just because she asked the way she did, I shout, "Hell yeah!"

"Since when?" she asks.

"Since forever!" I shout back, not knowing what to expect, was I gonna have to beat her ass or what? I stand 5'6 170 pounds, small waist, cute face, hips and thighs that come from that southern Cornbread, caramel skin toned looking so fresh and so clean but ready to get dirty, in my chic black silk-like shirt which drooped in the front to show my small 34C breast but fit just right around my stomach to show that it is flat enough for you to see how voluptuous my hips and thighs are in these stretch Parasuco's and black boots that help me shake what my mama gave me.

Then I get my girls Keisha, Nicole, and Kelly standing behind me, screw facing her. The club atmosphere adds tension to

1

the situation, especially when this is the segment of the night that they play all the down south fuck you and your crew songs. It also doesn't help that we have only been here for about an hour and me and my crew were basically drunk before we got here, plus on top of that this is my second blue motorcycle. She walks away to a table to put down her drink. In a restaurant turned club at night called Kamikaze's, the bar was located in the center of the room. The tables around the bar were the hottest spots to sit in, so we always grab those tables first. Sizing her up in my mind I notice she is about 5'9 130 pounds nice shape, nice outfit: white baby doll shirt flaring at the bottom, skin tight black jeans fitting to her modelesque physique. The thing that was most unattractive about her was her face, chocolate toned, ebony hair stretching a little past her shoulders just enough to match my length, long headed, fat jaws, not very pretty. At this point I prepare myself for a brawl when she comes back, but to my surprise she came back apologizing. Now I am confused.

"I am sorry, I don't usually approach the females I normally take it up with him," she began.

Stopping her there, I ask, "Who are you? Are you his girlfriend?"

"Yes!"

So I ask again, confused, "You are his girlfriend?"

This time the story changes. "Well no, but we are working things out."

I laugh, "You're working things out?"

"Yes," she says passionately, "he tells me he loves me and we are going to get back together."

Mitchell was across the bar at a table on the other side of the circle observing the whole situation but acting like he wasn't.6'4 240 pounds chocolate toned, sexy as hell, he had a laid back swagger that would make you want to embarrass yourself just to get his attention.

2

"Well, he's in the club too," I stutter to redirect my thinking from wanting to undress him back to what was going on. "Let's go talk to him."

"No, no, he's mad at me," she says.

Now I am really confused because she just told me he loves her and they are working it out but when I recommend that we go over and approach him she says he's mad at her. Squinting my eyes and balling up my eyebrows, I take a chance at hearing her out, then she starts asking me crazy questions, like do you sleep in his bed, does he take you out to eat.

"Look I am not telling you all that, it's none of your business."

"Well, I apologize but can you..." she pauses in the middle of her sentence and notices that he and I have an eye contact that is unbreakable. She apologizes again and walks away. Mitchell is sitting at a table alone so I walk over and have a seat.

"What did she say to you?" he asks when just then she walks up to the table and is staring at him with her back to me. My girls are watching from a short distance waiting for the signal to start throwing some bows.

So I yell, "Tell him everything you just told me, that he is telling you he loves you and y'all are working it out."

Mitchell stares at her with a you must be crazy look and asks, "When did I tell you I love you?"

Trinity, now in a state of shock and not knowing what to say, replies "Oh you don't tell me you love me, Mitchell?"

"WHEN!" Mitchell yells.

"Oh, I am gonna remember that!" she yells back as she storms out of the club.

He looks back at me and says, "Excuse me for a second, let me handle this." He grabs his Corona, gulps it down and walks out after her. I look up at a guy sitting at a table in the next section. He shakes his head and says, "That's crazy." I shake

3

my head in agreement and walk back over to my friends...not catching the reality of what just went down...not knowing that this was only the first of many dramatic incidents to happen during the relationship I had just started with Mitchell Austin.

CHAPTER 1.

Meet Celeste

As a 16-year-old 10th grader, I was a hard head doing what I wanted to do. My mom, Celine Bellamy, was an accountant by trade, but she didn't have a degree so she was always pressing me to go to college. She was about 5'7, light skinned, 170 pounds, with long dark hair. She married my dad a year before having me: Sylvester Bellamy, 6 foot, brown skinned with dark curly hair, he was a machine operator for one of the large banks in the area. About three years ago, my mom gave her life to Christ in a holiness church, which my younger brother, Shaun Bellamy, and I were forced to join, "Clean Spirit Holy Tabernacle." Shaun was 7 years younger than me. We got along fine but it was hard trying to explain things to him because he was so young.

Once my mom got saved, she decided that she would convert everyone in the house to what she would call a "true" Christian, a "holy person" living a "holy life" but my dad wasn't having it. During my middle school years, I went along with all of her newfound Christian rules. She became really strict on me all of a sudden. No music videos, no talking to boys on the phone, and blah blah blah. Basically I couldn't do any of the things that I had been able to do before. Things that had been cool before all of a sudden were not the "Christian way" according to my mom and her church.

It was hard trying to change my life to fit what she wanted. We went to church Tuesdays, Wednesdays, and twice on Sundays. These church services would last for hours: hours of jumping, shouting, hand clapping, and tambourine beating BS, if you ask me. The church didn't believe in wearing pants, makeup, or earrings and claimed that it was because the Bible said so. Therefore, I spent three years of my life looking totally different from all the other kids in school. I was picked on about my long skirts, which came to my ankles. We were a middle class family so my clothes weren't ragged but I was not rocking the high price name brands that some kids could. Instead of the white Air Force Ones I had white Keds with a Tweety Bird on the side.

I always felt like my mom wanted to get me better things but at the time we just couldn't afford it. I survived middle school with low self esteem but I was still happy because I thought I was doing what was right to please God or at least my mom. In all of my doubt and confusion about my mom's sudden 360 degree turn, I would often pray to ask God to help me deal with the low self esteem.

My dad was on drugs but he wasn't the pawn-your-TV type of drug addict. He must have been on something more expensive like cocaine because he only used the money needed for bills but I never really knew exactly. I would wake up several times during the night to arguments in a whispering tone between my mom and dad.

"I am sorry, this is the last time, Celine, I promise."

"You have said that so many times, Sylvester, when are you going to stop it," my mom would reply in a crying crackling voice.

Even though I was hearing all of these conversations I would remain silent about them during the day, but they were beating up on my self-esteem too. I was constantly asking, "God, is this why I can't get the shoes I want because of my dad and his habit? Can you help him, Lord, please because I really like those new all black Air Force Ones. Well, I know you can do it God, in Jesus name I pray. Amen." Getting up from my knees, pulling back my cover on my full size bed, which was pressed up against the far wall in my room. As you enter my room you automatically notice that it is painted a pinkish mauve color. Pink is my favorite color – it has the power to make me happy when I am sad.

As I was drifting off to sleep, my dad called out, "Celeste, you sleep yet?" He crept over and sat slowly on the edge of the bed next to me.

"Nah dad, wassup?"

"Is everything okay with you? I see you're kinda quiet around the house lately."

"I am okay Dad, it's just that..."

He cut me off in the middle of my sentence to say; "You know that I love you, right?"

"Yes, sir."

"All right." As he walked away from the bed he gets to the doorway, he looked to the right at a couple of dollars on my dresser. "Uh uh. I am going to just take these few dollars for tonight. I will get them back to you in the morning, okay baby?"

"Okay, dad," I sighed and turned to stare at the blank wall beside me, thinking some things will never change. I tried to explain to Shaun what was going on but he was too young to understand. Daddy would ask us for money only at select times of the month. I soon discovered through listening a little harder to those whispering arguments that my dad got paid twice a month. My mom got paid every two weeks so in between his pay periods he would ask us for the little bit of allowance that mama gave us.

"Celeste, can you buy me some candy?" my brother inquired on the way to the corner store.

"Where is your money that mama gave you?"

"Daddy asked me did I have any money and I gave it to him."

"How many times do I have to tell you? If Daddy ask you for some money tell him you don't have any."

"But I can't lie to Daddy," he responded in tears.

"Come on boy!" I said, pushing the back of his head and realizing that he is too young to understand. With my arm around his little shoulders I felt as if he is under my wing. I wanted to shelter him from any pain I may have been feeling. My dad would often fuss with my mom protecting my brother from attending church every day all day. There were many Sundays when he got to stay home and I had to go. He never stood up for me or fought to keep me home and I never understood why. I questioned God on this one too, "Does he love him more, God?" I knew God was there but he wasn't saying much.

So here I am done with middle school, now attending one of the most popular high schools in Montgomery, AL, George Washington Carver High School a.k.a Carver. Montgomery was one of those places where if you lived there all your life it seemed like it was the only city in the world. Montgomery was known for holding back the people who allowed it to hold them back. Not too many opportunities were there but there were a few historical sites there such as the King Memorial Baptist Church.

For me and my family, Montgomery was a great place to be. Some areas could be a little dangerous and there wasn't much to do but hang with friends. I didn't have many friends in middle school because I was looked at as different. I always had family who attended school with me so I didn't feel alone. I was blessed with the gift of gab and I convinced people that wearing these skirts all the time was cool.

I spent 9th grade answering questions about my religion. "Why do you wear those long skirts?" Whispers in the hallway during the change of class, "There is that girl that wears skirts all the time." The summer after 9th grade I decided to take charge over my own life.

"I don't want to go to church today, Mom," I said one Sunday in an I-think-I-am-sick voice.

"What's wrong, you sick?"

"Nah, I just don't want to go."

"That's not good enough, you're going."

Smacking my lips I stumped into my room to get dressed but now I realized that church was my life. Between Sunday school, first Sunday service, second Sunday service, bible study, and prayer service I had no social life. People at school thought I was weird because of how religious I was and I was starting to side with them.

As my 10th grade year began, I was starting to feel like taking some independence. I rebelled hard against everything my mom and dad asked. I hooked up with a crew of four girls, which became more important to me than my family: Katrina, Stacy, Casey, and Eva. Katrina and I were the closest. That was my partner in crime. If you saw me you saw her. Eva was jealous of the relationship between me and Katrina. I never understood why she felt that way. It was weird because she had some kind of effect on Katrina. Stacy was the comedian of the crew but had the most attitude – she would always buck the system and act up in school. I never understood it because she was the most afraid of her parents. Casey was very promiscuous. Her mom had a tight leash on her so when she got out of her mom's sight she would grab hold of the first boy she could find. Eva was sneaky and would not be around often, but when she came around Katrina would follow her lead. Stacy, Casey, and I would bring this to Katrina's attention by joking (in Eva's absence of course).

"Hey, what are you guys doing this weekend?" Stacy would say to spark a lunch conversation. Our cafeteria was your average high school café: we had a choice of chicken, pizza, or the regular nasty school lunch. We had the option of eating inside or there was a nice landscaped area where people could eat outside. This is where the white skateboarders usually ate and smoked a pack of cigarettes a day behind a great big oak tree.

"It's whatever with me, wassup?" Casey answered.

"Well, I hear that there is this house party Saturday night in North Montgomery." Katrina and I were at full attention while Stacy gives the details of the party.

"Well, Katrina may have to ask her mama Eva if it's okay," I snarled as I strategize on the next french fry I will eat.

Casey laughed and said, "Yeah, you know she has to get permission."

"Yeah she can't do anything without Eva," Stacy cosigned.

We all laughed but Katrina wasn't laughing as hard as we were. Eva would always persuade Katrina to do things against what we already had planned. Eva would often come up at the last minute and get Katrina to change plans with us to hang with her but I was overlooking this and carrying on business as usual.

They introduced me to selling weed, boosting, and hanging out. I was starting to lean towards being more like them than like the "holy person" my mom planned for me to be. God was still important to me, though. I felt so guilty about everything that I did that I would pray before doing bad things and repent after doing them. "Lord, keep me safe while I am out here smoking this weed. Lord, please don't let me get caught boosting today. Lord, please forgive me for what I am doing," and those were just a few of my constant talks with God.

School became less and less important, the things that my crew thought were cool, I did, and the things they didn't,

I didn't. They had become my family, they understood me, Katrina and I felt the same way about everything. Stacy and Casey were good sources for making you feel better after a shitty week. Stacy and I were the only ones in the group to have both parents still together. I guess that's why Stacy was afraid of acting up too much. For me, home could be hell some nights but I was proud that my parents were still together. The whispering arguments were never ending, but me coming home high drowned most of them out. Life became less and less important, I was now hooked on weed and my parents were trying to do all they could to constrain me. They may not have been able to work together on my dad's drug problem but when it came to me they were a united front, however, I had no respect for my dad.

"Celeste, you need to focus and stop smoking so much," my dad would snarl when I would come home high.

"How can you talk about me when you are on something yourself?"

"Hold on now, Celeste!" screamed my mom from her room to mine. My mom often had to break up the arguments between me and my dad. I rolled my eyes and stomped into my room. We never closed our doors because that's just how my mom ran the house. There was an open door policy but if I could have slammed my door I would have. In school, I was always talking back to teachers and skipping class. Those teachers didn't know my struggle; I was a low self-esteemed child of a drug addict and a Jesus freak. My parents figured that they had to take some action so they would put me on punishment. So what, I would sneak out of the house, lie about where I had been, and the awesome part about it was I didn't care. Stacy and I would steal clothes and sell them at school. Casey and Katrina would sell weed at school and a little in the streets to people we knew. We were family, and any profit that came into the family was split with the people

11

who made it. Eva joined us at times and put us on to most of the weed connections. She also knew some employees at different stores that would overlook us while we got what we wanted. Everything stayed even and everybody pulled their weight. Katrina's mom was crazy enough to buy her a car for her 16th birthday so we were doing what we wanted to do.

My boyfriend at the time, Teddy, was one of power on the West End of town. We were regulars with him and his crew. They would give us weed to sell for them sometimes and I ran packages for him during lunchtime with Katrina's car. I was on top of my game I had all the newest clothes and shoes. This was something I had never had before, 135 pounds. Standing 5'4 caramel brown, long dark brown hair, Parasuco's were the only jeans I thought I'd ever wear, they fit just right along all of my curves. I threw out all those old long skirts; I was making my own money so I was buying my own clothes. I had also become a professional booster so having the freshest clothes was nothing. I would sneak around, date, and talk to boys on the phone. My parents were always tripping, putting me on punishments that required me to stay in my room unless I had to use the bathroom. I laughed at that. As soon as they went to sleep I would have Katrina come and get me from the street behind our house. Our parents couldn't handle us. We were constantly high and living life to the fullest, having fun.

On one report card I had missed like 30 days out of one class. Our school was a big two story white building with an all glass front. It looked more like a coliseum than a high school. There was a parking lot for students in the back of the building and the faculty parked in the front and on the right side of the building. There were three entrances, one in the back of the building, one on the right side of the building which connected the parking lots on the front and side, and, of course, the front entrance. We lived about five minutes away from the school so my mom would drop me off on her way to work.

This particular morning, Katrina and I planned to leave school early to hit the mall up and get high. It was the middle of 10th grade year sometime around January. Stepping out of my mom's car that morning the air was crisp but the plan was in place and school was not on my mind.

"Aight, Ma!" I yelled back as I slammed the door. She and I were not friends – she was like my enemy always trying to hold me back. Since we entered school grounds from the back of the building she drove around the right side of the building to drop me off at the side entrance and to exit the grounds from the front entrance. As I walked up to the side glass door, I opened it as if I really wanted to enter, when Katrina pulled up at the curbside in front of where I was standing.

"Hey! Let's ride."

Looking back at her over my right shoulder holding the door handle in my right hand, I smiled, "Let's do it!" I hopped in the car and we carried out business as usual. Getting home that night I was satisfied with my day. I had made about $150 and I was high as hell. Sticking my key in the door I wasn't ready for what was waiting for me.

"Hey, wassup Ma, Dad!" I yelled to them as I walk past them to attempt to believe that I hadn't been the topic of conversation for the last hour.

"Don't wassup me!" started my mom.

High as a kite my mind is too slow to think about the possibilities of what she could be talking about now. In my head I started to question myself, did I not clean the kitchen, did another one of my teachers call, what the hell did I do now? The high from the weed made me put the moment on pause as I gathered my thoughts. Once I couldn't figure it outI pressed play in my mind by screaming, "What are you talking about?"

"As I was exiting the school grounds this morning I looked back in my rear view mirror to see you getting into a dark

13

green Volkswagen beetle."

That was Katrina's car, we called it "The Cricket." It was an old-school car but her boyfriend from the West End put some rims on it and it got us where we needed to go.

"I don't know what you are talking about, Ma."

"You don't know what I am talking about!?" SLAP! Across my left cheek she laid down what she thought was a hand of power but for me became a hand of vengeance, swinging back toward her with the back of my right hand we started to tussle.

As we fell to the floor my dad jumped in to pick me up and slam me on the couch, screaming, "Have you lost your damn mind? Give me the phone, I am calling Katrina's mom."

Mad as hell and breathing as if fire was coming out of my nose, I stomped into my room, slammed the door, and laid on the bed. This was the first sense of emotion I had felt this school year. I was disappointed in myself that I had hit my mom but I felt even more gangsta, wait till I tell this story at 2nd lunch tomorrow.

Morning came just like it did every other day. Regardless of things that happened the night before it was understood in our family that the routine didn't change. You got dressed and Mama took you to school. My dad worked third shift so he would be getting home as we were leaving out, that was mornings that he did come home. You never knew when that would happen...the drugs had him stuck in a zone where no one could reach him. He and I were bumping heads constantly. He would call me naive, stupid, and he even called me a bitch once, but in my mind he was a crack head even though I wasn't sure if he was even on crack. As usual, I got out of the car but yelled a little softer and with a different attitude, "Aight, Ma" as I slammed the door.

For some reason she dropped me off at the front entrance this time. As I walked in to the front door, it was like walking into high school in heaven, everything was all white and the morning rising sun gave everything a bright white glare. To the left was the office and straight ahead was the stairwell to first period. I walked the steps anticipating seeing Katrina in my first class of the day, writing notes back and forth about what happened last night the whole 55-minute period. As I reached the top of the stairs there was a set of double doors, pulling the one on the right to enter I see Katrina and Eva coming down the hallway. Eva's hand was on Katrina's shoulder and she was whispering to her as they walked. I stand just behind the double doors and they approach me.

"You cut back!" Katrina yelled.

"WHAT! What the hell are you talking about?" I yelled back.

"You cut back, you are a snitch."

"Hell no, that's not what happened, let me talk to you for a second," meaning I didn't want to talk to her in front of Eva.

"We don't have time for this," Eva said as she pushed Katrina through the left side of the double doors past me. She looked back with a snarl of a grin and kept walking. From that day forth there was beef between me and my so-called "crew." We were separated in an instant and I was now all alone again. Katrina and Eva convinced everybody else in the crew that I was a snitch and in the hood that's one of the worst things you can do.

I tried to look at the bright side of things. If I could just avoid them everything would be cool. I was making progress avoiding them until I remembered that we had band class together. All five of us were in the band together as flag girls. This was the hardest period of the day to endure because I had to sit all alone or with the lames.

Luckily for me, the rest of the day was cool, because I had family that went to school with me. My mother's side of the family was real close and I had a cousin on every grade level

15

at the high school. We were always close, riding to school to-gether. I would go to my cousin's after school every day. So I started hanging with them more and more during the school day. I was still my usual self, boosting but now I had a job. My aunt Lisa was the head manager at a McDonalds, so every teenager on my mom's side of the family automatically had a job at the age of 15. Now that some of my connections were dead I needed a job to keep up my lavish lifestyle. Getting my hair and nails done every two weeks, getting the newest Jordan's every time they came out.

In band class one day, things got a little heated. Entering the band room there was a short hallway with a concrete floor up until you reached the band room itself, which was light blue, carpeted and set up like a college band room. Three levels of band room chairs and music stands but it used to be our favorite place. We could show off and be us, we could dance and twirl our flags and act a fool and no one could stop us. We would practice every day and anticipate getting out there on the football field on Friday nights and be able to march to the beat of the bass drum and dance to the sound of the trumpet.

About two weeks after Katrina and I stopped being friends I am feeling better and getting used to not hanging with them. I would run into them on the West Side sometimes but band class was the only time we were forced to be in the same room for a period of time. I entered the band room that day with my head up feeling good. I was attending school more regularly and my grades were coming up slowly but sure-ly. Today was free day; we would usually have those after straight practicing for a couple of weeks. I was sitting on one side of the band room, writing in my notebook as usual. Being without best friends made me write even more, my notebook was my friend.

"Yeah well, she got a job now, she need to give me my

money," I heard Katrina saying to Eva.

"Well, you need to get it from her then," Stacy cosigned.

I heard them chatting but I was paying them no attention. I was thinking, "Is she seriously over there talking shit about $5 that I didn't even know I owed her?" I looked up at Casey who was staring at me during their conversation. I smirked, put my head down, and continued writing.

"I think you need to go ask her for your money," said Casey.

"Okay, it's almost time to go kids get your things together, place all instruments back in their place," announced the band director. Everybody started to crowd in the short hallway to wait for the bell to ring.

As I was entering the hallway to go and stand with every body else, "Uh Celeste, Katrina called.

I threw my backpack over my right shoulder as I turned and asked, "WHAT!"

Standing about 20 steps away from me, she yelled, "Remember when I loaned you that $5 at footlocker that time because you was short on your Timbs? I need to know if you got that money."

Now I was looking confused. But I did remember when that happened and it happened sometime the last year, so now I was irritated that she even thought to ask me about this.

"No, but when I get it I will give it to you," I answered with an attitude. She started to turn back to talk to the crew when I couldn't just let it go, I had to give her a piece of my mind. "And look, if you got something to say to me you can just come over and say it to my face, don't be all on the other side of the room talking shit."

Dropping her back pack, "Well wassup!"

I dropped my back pack, "WASSUP!"

We ran towards each other and met at about ten steps brawling. I blanked out once I reached her. I just kept throw-

17

ing my hands and she was throwing hers. It's funny, though, because I don't remember her touching me or me touching her, but according to everybody else we were definitely hitting each other. A couple of the band guys broke it up. The crew ran out with Katrina to avoid getting suspended and I ran to get one of my oldest cousins because I wasn't driving, but I was stopped in the hallway by one of the assistant principals. Both me and Katrina got ten days out-of-school suspension.

Now my parents thought I was going back to my old ways. I had to start back going to church again but not as much, only on Sundays. Even though I hated going, it wasn't half bad as long as I only had to go one day and didn't have to wear long skirts all the time.

I had been dating one of the guys at school for a while now. It's 11th grade and he had been liking me since the end of my 9th grade year. I would sneak and talk to him on the phone while my mom was gone. I was still a virgin and the guys that knew that all wanted to be my first, including him. His name was DJ, 6'3 190 pounds soaking wet, he was fairly skinny but tall, caramel skin toned and had a heart of gold. He just didn't have a focus for life. He was about three years older than me and still not out of high school. He was doing the same things I was doing, skipping school and getting high. He also worked at a McDonalds on the other side of town.

After I was separated from my crew I started to be with him more and focusing on school more, but money was taking precedence over all of that. I continued boosting and getting high every day all day. When people wanted the fresh clothes they knew where to come. I was looking fresh myself and still cool with everybody but my old crew. Now I would smoke and hang with a different crowd. Junior year, only one more year until I get out of this hell hole and get a real job. I had no idea what I wanted to do but I wanted to get out of high school. All odds seemed to be against me and I didn't care.

I had missed almost the whole year out of my Latin and biology classes. I sweet talked my teachers into working with me on my grades so I could graduate, but my biology teacher was not trying to hear it. I wasn't really a disrespectful child when I was in class – going to class was the problem. My biology teacher would tell me that I would have to come if I wanted her help. I would agree, then I would say whatever.

I was feeling like I was maturing now. I was interested in having sex so I went to my mom for birth control. "Ma, uh, I need to talk to you," I stuttered as I walked into her bedroom one night. We lived in a three bedroom, two bathroom one level house in a predominately black but nice neighborhood. When you walk in the front door the kitchen was to the right, straight ahead was the living room and dining area. To the left, along that left wall was the bathroom, my room, my brother's room, and then down at the end of the hallway was my parents' room. In the hallway leading to my parents' room was the wash room on the right. Walking down the hall that day I stopped at the wash room and almost didn't enter the room to have this conversation because I had a feeling it would not go too well.

"Sure, what would you like to talk about, Celeste?" my mom answered.

Clearing my throat, I really didn't know how to ask, so I just blurted out, "Ma, I want some birth control."

"WHAT!"

I dropped my head and braced myself as if to expect another slap.

"Well, I will have to pray about it first, Celeste, and I will let you know." Every time she talked to me she had to say my name as if to let me know how disappointed she was about everything I had done.

"Okay," I said in a confused manner, not understanding why the Lord would have to give her permission to give me birth

19

control. "What does prayer have to do with it?" I mumbled as I stump down the hall.

"WHAT!" she yelled.

"Huh, nothing." I replied. Well, while she was praying spring break rolled around and I couldn't wait any longer. I walked over to DJ's house, which was about a five-minute walk through the streets behind my house. One thing led to another and I was on my back on top of a full size mattress with noisy springs, looking up at a cracked ceiling. His house was an older house, hardwood floors all the way through, three bedrooms, one bathroom and one level. I was nervous and excited all at the same time. He kissed me slow on the lips, then down to my neck and up to my ears. I was thinking, I didn't even know a kiss on the ear could make me feel this way but I was starting to relax and like it. Rubbing his hand under my shirt and up to my right breast he lifts my shirt and kisses my nipple, caressing them with his tongue. I am feeling a way that I have never really felt before, he was taking it slow and being a gentleman about it, But at the moment, "How the hell do I know if he's doing it right this is an inauguration for me," I chuckled to myself. "Be serious, Celeste, this is really happening."

I was thinking so much that I couldn't even focus on the fact that he was taking my pants and panties off, so I helped him out a little with them. He threw them to the side and lay back down on top of me. As he put it halfway in I started to feel a pain as if my vagina was stretching wide enough to fit in a nice sized cucumber. I didn't want to let him know I was scared and in pain so I relaxed my pelvic muscles and closed my eyes tightly. More thinking, "Is this what all the excitement is all about?" I was focusing on getting it over with but it had just begun. I was keeping my legs relaxed and holding my breath.

"Do you want me to get the condom?"

Laying there trying to bear the pain, the sound of his voice startled me. I didn't know how to answer. It was feeling okay without a condom but I never knew what a condom felt like in the first place. I had heard that it was better without one. "Nah, it's okay, I guess," I whispered back in an attempt to just speed this up so we can get this over with. He carried on for about 10 minutes, which seemed to be the longest 10 minutes of my life. I could feel some substance rushing down my leg, which I later learned was blood meaning that my hymen was broken.

Now I had experienced sex and was no longer a virgin, what was all the hype about? I continued to do it but through a sex education class at school, I learned the importance of condoms and I used them from then on out. I was barely making it through my 11th grade year but I was making it. My school had a program that was called "extended day." It was open to people from any school in the county and was for students like me who needed to make up some classes.

One morning before school I found myself feeling really sick. My first instinct was to go to the bathroom. I sat on the toilet to do number 2 but a feeling in my gut caused me to jump up and turn around. I started to gag as if I was throwing up, nothing was coming out but this yellow slimy looking substance. At that point, I remembered the stories from one of my older cousins, Toot, who had her daughter when she was in middle school. That day at school I told her about my episode that morning, after school we planned to get me a test. Toot, one of my other cousins, Meka, and I went to a nearby drug store immediately after school. We could not go to either one of our houses to take the test because we didn't want any evidence laying around that our parents could find. Beside the drug store was a Subway Sandwich Shop, which would be perfect since it had a private bathroom. I urinated on the stick, placed it back of the toilet in the protective cover, then

21

called them into the bathroom to wait for the results. We were all crowded up beside the bathroom sink and anticipating the results. "NO!!!" I yelled as Meka and Toot just gasped in excitement, fear, and shock. The test was positive. What was I going to do? My mom was holier than thou, my dad was a cocaine addict who could care less about me right now. I was nervous all the way home.

We rode in silence until we reached the left turn to get into my neighborhood. Toot advocates that I tell my mom, if I didn't she was going to tell. Knowing my mom, abortion is not an option and who knows what my dad will say now. A couple of days went by and I am still trying to hide this. Every day I was trying to avoid Toot so she wouldn't ask me about it, which was hard being that I went to her house every day after school to wait for my mom to pick me up.

One morning while I was throwing up, my little brother started banging on the door. "Hurry up, get out of the bathroom!" At this time he was about 10 years old and I wanted to beat his ass for making my spot hot.

"Wait a minute!" Before I could blurt out another word I was throwing up again.

"Are you okay?" he asked in a more calm voice.

"Yeah! Leave me alone."

"Okay," running down the hall shouting "Mama, Mama I think Celeste is throwing up."

"UH! I hate him!" I yelled to myself.

Tap, tap, tap on the door my mom yelled softly, "ARE YOU OK IN THERE?"

I gathered strength to flush the toilet, grab a wash cloth, wipe my mouth, and open up the door. "Yeah I am fine," I replied to brush her off and slid past her into my room. Sitting on the bed I was still feeling a little weak from all the throwing up.

"Are you pregnant, Celeste?" Looking up at her I couldn't

22

even lie to her and how the hell did she know. After all the other things I had done she at least deserved to know the truth about this one.

"Yeah Ma, I am pregnant."

Her mouth dropped, she turned in silence, and walked down the hall to her room. There was silence the whole morning all the way to school. Walking into those glass doors that day was a difficult thing to do. I had to tell DJ. During first period he would always hang out at the gym. I saved the test and had it in my pocket ready to show him I was for real. My biggest fear was that he would say, "It's not mine." I would be devastated. He was sitting with a group of friends.

"DJ! Can I talk to you for a minute?" I yelled out to him.

Quickly separating from his friends he could see a troubled look in my eyes, he hugged me as soon as he was in distance to do so. "Wassup? Everything ok?"

"Ah, not really, pulling out the test with the positive test results his mouth drops.

"You, you, are pregnant?" he stuttered.

"Yes, and it's yours." We decided to leave for the day. We went back to his house. His mom worked first shift, but my mom worked first and my dad worked third so someone was always at home at my house. His house was the perfect place to run to. We lay in his bed all day talking about what our plan was.

"If you want to have it then it's cool. If you don't want to have it I understand, I want what will be best for you." He stressed that this was his stance on the topic.

"I know my mom will not stand for abortion. It would be against all she believes, but I am not sure that I really want to have a baby. A baby, DJ, what will we do with a baby?"

"We will just have to figure that out, babe." I curled up into his arms, buried my head in his chest, and slept until school was out. At home that night there was tension in the air. My mom and dad were in the room with the door closed and I know I was the topic of conversation this time.

"Celeste!" my mom called out to me to come into the room. I quickly pushed a big gulp of saliva down my throat and walked down the hallway. I sat on the bed close to my mom for protection from whatever my dad was going to throw at me.

My dad started ranting and raving, "How the hell did you let this happen, Celine? We are not having a baby in this house, God dammit!"

"Sylvester, clearly we cannot kill a baby," my mom rebutted.

"So you think she should have this bastard child!?" he asked my mom in a condescending tone.

"Yes, I will not let her have an abortion, I don't believe in it!" she yelled back.

"I will have nothing to do with it, I will not love it, I will not touch it, I don't even want to see it!" He ended the conversation by walking out of the room and grabbing a beer from the fridge. Somehow I held in my tears until I got to my bed. I showered and went to bed as usual. In the middle of the night I was awakened from a different sound. This wasn't the usual whispering arguments but more of a whimper. I got up out of bed and went to the living room, it was about 1:00 a.m. so my dad hadn't been long left for work. It was my mom on the couch in the living room crying.

I sat beside her and began to cry also. "I am sorry Mama, I am so sorry." We hugged each other and cried together. This was the first step in the restoration of our relationship. From then on my world was changed. I had already rebelled as much as I could and bumped heads with my mom so much that at this point she let up her thump from my head and allowed me to make my own decisions. I had a baby on the way now I had to get myself together and get out of high school.

I attended summer school between my junior and senior years to make up my math grade. I gained a new group of friends and my cousins had become my crew. My grades got better, I stopped skipping school, smoking weed, and boosting. I had a baby on the way I have to make a better life for it. DJ and I were together most of the time, if I wasn't in extended day or with my mom. He was my refuge, I needed his touch, his kiss, his love. However, nothing changed on his end. He still didn't have a plan for his life. He was too old to continue high school, he had to take a GED class at either at Montgomery Technical College or at Carver, in the night school program that was during the same times as extended day. He seemed to be doing great in the GED class but he couldn't keep it up, between working at McDonalds and a little hustling during the day he stopped attending the GED classes. My body is feeling different, my stomach was stretching, my breast was sore, I was always hot and irritated. I was crying over stupid things like commercials.

"I am ready for this baby to come out, DJ!"

"Babe, it's ok."

"But look at me, I am getting fat and my shape is gone."

"I still love it girl, don't worry about it." Nine months passed by very slow, during which 11th grade ended and 12th grade began. I finished with C's and D's on my report card, I just barely made it. I started 12th grade with ambition and I was determined to make the little time I had left to do better in school count. Before I knew it, it was December 1999 and it was time for my little baby girl to arrive. My dad who hadn't spoken to me since that conversation in their bedroom that night came by the hospital. I felt happy for a second until I realized that he didn't come to see me. He walked into the room, said a couple of words to my mom and left. When I was feeling sad for a moment, DJ saw me staring and understood the sadness in my eyes. He grabbed my hand and I relaxed.

Laying my head back on the hospital pillow with a blank mind, I had know idea how I was going to make this work, thinking about the things my dad was saying and I started to think they were true. I have no business having a baby, my life is over for sure.

It was a week after my due date and my baby wasn't trying to come out. They had given me medicine to induce my labor about 30 minutes before the doctor walked up to my bedside with a strut that just said I have bad news. "We have been monitoring the baby and her heart rate is kind of low and we will need to perform a c-section. She will be better off if we get her out versus us inducing your labor."

I began to cry, looking up at DJ he kissed my cheek and held my hand tighter. "It will be ok."

The doctor is looking at us like we are crazy, and asks "What are you crying for?" in a very nonchalant tone.

"Because I don't want to have an operation!" I yelled at him.

"Things will be perfectly fine," he replied. I was irritated by the doctor's attitude but hell, what was I going to do about it?

At 11:52 a.m. on New Year's Eve out popped Ashley Onye' Bellamy, my reason for living. It was the happiest moment of my life and DJ's too. He had a sparkle in his eyes as he held her more than he would let me. He only went home for a few hours a day. He stayed in the room with me the entire time I was in the hospital. I started to look at him different, he was not just my boyfriend, he is my daughter's father. He loved me and I loved him. We were starting our family. I exhaled with that thought in mind and I knew that things were the way they were supposed to be.

After leaving the hospital I was home schooled for about 6 weeks. When I returned to school there was not much time left in the school year. DJ kept Ashley while I went to school.

I was feeling great, things were back on track, and I actually had a chance at going to college.

"College, Ma?"

"I want you to apply for a couple of colleges close by, they don't have to be in Montgomery if you want to go to a school outside of Montgomery."

"How will I go to school, Ma, I have Ashley? Maybe I should just get a regular job and live here."

"NO! Your dad and I will work out how to keep Ashley, I want you to have a good education."

"Ok, Ma, well, I will take the SAT next Saturday at 8am."

I was hyped about taking the SAT and the possibility of going to college was overwhelming. I didn't do the greatest on the SAT but my mom pushed every application to every historically black college or university in our area. Finally, a response came from Tuskegee University, it was in Tuskegee, Alabama, about 30 minutes away from Montgomery. My mom was so excited and agreed to keep my daughter while I attended school.

Tuskegee would be perfect, away from home but close enough where I could go home anytime to see my baby. I noticed that my dad was coming around. He would sneak into my room at night and peak at us when he thought I was sleeping, he would go in and kiss my daughter in her crib while I was out of the room. After a couple of weeks we started to talk again and he fell in love with my daughter. She was his baby. You couldn't take her out of the house with out him asking a thousand questions. Words screamed in fury and misunderstanding had now turned into acceptance and love. Since the day I found out I was pregnant my life was changed. I shouldn't have let myself have to have a baby to get focused in life but here I was another statistic for now, but my mother and I were determined to turn that around. My dad was still on drugs, at this point I found that it was cocaine and maybe some crack every now and then.

Things had gotten a little worse around the house. High school graduation was a release from past tensions for me. I had come a long way and it took an 8 pound little girl named Ashley to turn my whole world around. DJ sat with my family at the graduation and held Ashley pointing to me in the crowd. All I could do was smile. My mom planned a summer vacation to Paramount's Carowinds since I was going off to school. My mom rented two of the new Nissan Altima's and we were set to leave on Saturday morning. Coming home from my cousin's house that day I noticed that one of the rental cars was missing.

"Aight, Toot, see you later!" I yelled as I stepped out of her mom's van. I looked up at my house with the sun shining in my face and Ashley throwed over my shoulder under a blanket. I sensed trouble in the camp. My house had white vinyl siding, three windows in the front, starting at the left corner, one window for my room, one window for the main bathroom, and one for the kitchen. We had a glass screen door and a white door to match the siding. I stepped into the house and things appeared to be ok. I continued with my normal evening rituals feeding and bathing the baby. My little brother played outside until it was dark. My mom was quiet and seemed sorta frantic but she could do a good job hiding her feelings. Ashley went to sleep and I jumped on the opportunity to sleep when she was sleeping, I had everything prepared for our big day tomorrow.

"Celeste, wake up, wake up," my mom said, shoving me frantically.

"Okay Ma, wassup?"

"We are going to South Carolina to Carowinds for our trip tonight, we will go down and get a hotel room and he will not spoil this! We will take this trip!"

"Ma, what are you talking about?" I screamed as I grabbed

her wrist gently.

Her eyes were stretched wide as if she had been in shock. "Your father has not been home since he supposedly went to check on something at work at 12:00am Friday morning, we are going on this trip, he will not ruin this."

Without question I got up and gathered my things. My brother, who never liked to go to sleep anyway, walked out of his room curious. "Ma, wassup?!"

My mom walked right pass him down the hallway as if she didn't even hear him. "We are going to South Carolina tonight, Shaun, get your stuff together." I said.

"YYEEESS!!!" he replied, running back into his room to get ready. My mom was in her room searching for something. I peaked down the hall into her room and her search had ended with some hidden money. We packed the car, jumped on the road, and ended up in South Carolina at a Ramada Inn. As my mom stuck the key card into the room slot it was like she was opening her passage to freedom. She laid on the first of two double beds and exhaled, as if she had temporarily run away from something. My brother and I had no clue as to how much our mom was really going through. I overlooked those whispering arguments and my mom was so supportive of me that I thought everything was cool. I ignored days my daddy stayed out all night and just came to the conclusion that this was just him. However, we had the best weekend ever. My aunt and a couple of people from church came down to join us.

Returning back home on Sunday, the car had been returned and my dad had returned with it. I was expecting all hell to break lose when we stepped foot in the door that day. It was a beautiful day and the sun always seemed to bounce off of our house and directly into your eyes as you pulled up to it. Stepping inside of the glass door, my dad was sitting on the couch looking at TV, smoking a cigarette. My mom stopped at the front door and stared at him. I hurried my brother into the

29

room with me to help me unpack and get the baby settled.

"Look, I will get my sister to take me to take the cars back," my mom said in a stern voice."

"Aight," my dad replied in a high unexpected tone. I was surprised, my mom didn't scream on him. She showed that she was getting fed up, my dad was in panic but didn't know how to show it. Later that night he came into my room before going to work.

"Celeste, are you awake?"

"Yes, Daddy."

"I am sorry, baby," he whispered. "I am sorry, she is going to leave me for sure."

"Daddy!" I yelled softly to stop him, "she has been there this long, I don't think she will leave you now."

"You know that I love you baby?"

"Yes, Daddy." Kissing my forehead he exited my room and went to work. I truly didn't understand why my mom stayed with him, but I knew she would never leave. He is my dad and I loved him, I repeated in my mind as my tears comforted me as I went to sleep.

Soon it was time for me to go off to school. We arranged for DJ to keep Ashley during the day and my parents would get her at night. My dad changed shifts on his job and everything was set. I went off to school to experience something new and far greater than what Montgomery had to offer. I let go of all the friends and drama from high school and focused on a new life. Of course, my family and I remained close no matter what.

Freshman year, we moved everything into my dorm room. Barbee Hall, it was an eight story brick building that looked like a prison. When you walked into the dorm past the lobby, there were these double glass doors leading to a courtyard...if you looked up you could see straight up to the sky. The balconies of the dorm rooms formed a perfect rectangular spiral

30

leading up to the top floor.

I was excited and rushed to my room to meet my roommate. Her name was Shani, she was about 5'6/5'7, dark skinned, a little heavy set, she had her hair up in braids, micros I think, which I later learned was her style. She was cool from the first day and everything was cool. I found myself actually happy, I pushed all of my past to the back of my mind and started a future. I designed my schedule to get done with my classes early in the morning. I lost about 20 pounds just by walking across campus every day. I made new friends through Shani. Back home things were not what I had hoped they'd be. My mom and dad were having a lot of problems. My mom was giving my dad an ultimatum: "I have spent too many years dealing with your bullshit, Sylvester. I have applied for a job working with my niece in Maryland."

"What?! Maryland!"

"Yes, Maryland, if you want to move together, then get it together!" Now mama was not playing. Shaun was now about 11 and starting to see and hear the things I tried to explain to him before, but I wasn't there to explain and comfort him like I wanted too. I was 30 minutes away experiencing independence and life.

DJ and I were growing apart. He was taking care of Ashley and being a great father but as far as our relationship, I couldn't see it going anywhere. He had not obtained his GED, and he was still working at little fast food restaurants here and there. Ashley had pampers, bottles, milk, clothes, and everything she needed. But for me it wasn't about Ashley anymore. I was in school seeing all these guys trying to do something with their life. Trying to get an education, working and getting educated, and these were black men. I was impressed. After giving things much thought I expressed my feelings to DJ and we broke up the second semester of my freshman year.

"DJ, I need to talk to you."

31

"Celeste, I already know what you are going to say. I have noticed for a while a change in you, you are growing up, experiencing new things."

"But DJ," I tried to rebut.

"No, Celeste, I understand and I want you to be happy."

From that day forward we went back to being friends again, I was now a single parent. DJ was in full support but we were no longer in a relationship. Coming home for the summer after my first year of college was not what I expected. I was a different person, I was more focused on what to do with my life. College gave me an open door for a new mind and a new life. My mom was offered a job in Maryland so she took it, she would drive 4 hours back home on Friday and back to Maryland on Sunday, but during the week she was not there. My dad was doing better with his drug problem because now he had to stay home with Ashley at night. My brother and my dad had a great hand in raising Ashley. It was like two men and a baby, changing diapers, bathing her, and feeding her.

However, our household was breaking apart and none of us was noticing it or we were trying to suppress it. When Mama went off to work during the week, I wondered what the hell is going on. "Shaun, is Mom and Dad together or are they separating?"

"I honestly don't know, Celeste, but it's crazy, I hear them arguing over the phone but I just go outside with my friends or close my door and play video games."

"I feel you, well, it will all be okay." When we were little we used to always have these conversations about if Mama and Daddy broke up who would we go with. I said Mama because she was more stable, and he said Daddy because he would never really punish us. But Shaun would always say that he felt that he should go with Mama as her protection. We laughed those conversations off feeling as if it was impossible for them to separate. Never say never I guess, because it looked like they were separating for sure.

Sophomore year is rolling around and I chose to stay in student housing that was off campus. It was only around the corner and my friend Jeronica who stayed next door had a car. I met Jeronica through Shani. She was about 5'9, dark skinned, and she had a short mushroom style haircut. She was not fat but not skinny; if there is an in between she was it. She and Shani were the nicest people I had ever met. I could trust them, they understood me the way that I only thought my crew from high school could. I realized that I was on a different level now, now I was on a positive level. Shani and I agreed to be roommates one last time since we had so much fun freshman year. Living off campus was cool, it was easy to break the co-ed rules.

Our housing was an old renovated motel called the Tuskegee Inn. It was nice enough for students and we felt like we had more freedom. Jeronica and Shani were into meeting guys on the Internet. This was something that I was definitely not into. Jeronica met this guy who was in the military, based on Maxwell-Gunter Air Force Base in Montgomery.

One night she gathered us together in her room with hopes that this guy was cute and plus he had some friends coming over with him. We were drinking and playing cards, when I noticed that one of his friends has a bottle of Moet. "Want to taste this, ladies?" he asked. His name was Damari, he was about 5'10, light skinned, he had a southern hood attitude with a smooth type of swagger. He was the cutest one besides Jeronica's man. Shani and I tasted the Moet and it was pretty good. That was my first time tasting it. He was feeling me and I was feeling him. The Moet had me feeling nice after about three cups straight. I had never really been a drinker so my tolerance was very low. He whispered in my ear, "I will pay you $50 to let me eat your pussy right now." I smiled but looked at him like nigga you must be stupid.

33

I hadn't had much experience with sex before college so this didn't amuse me but as a college student $50 for pleasure didn't sound bad. So I called Shani outside of the room to consult with her. I told her the proposition and she was like hell why not. She was tipsy too but we were broke ass college students and as long as it wasn't intercourse I didn't feel like I was selling myself. So I said yes, he and I went next door to my room and the games began.

"I am not having sex with you," I stressed more than once as I undressed from the bottom down.

"Okay, cool, it's cool," he replied. However, things changed when the clothes came off. "Just let me stick it in for a second."

"NO!"

"Just let me put the head in."

"NO!"

After a five-minute struggle I said okay. At this point things took a turn for the best, we began kissing very passionately, he slapped on some protection and his thrust was strong, rough, and big enough to make me gasp for air. Now this was what sex is all about! I actually had my first experience of what an orgasm was. When it came about I couldn't move, I felt like all of the fluids in my body were rushing through to my vagina and afterward I just laid there motionless, speechless, and wanting him to get out. He didn't even cum, but I think he realized the state that I was in and he laid down beside me. I laid in his arms, but when he fell asleep, I slid away, dug into his pockets and grabbed $100. I hid it in the closet then I woke him up, "Uh, Damari, you have to go back to Jeronica's room now. Shani is ready to come in and go to bed."

He didn't respond; he was too in a daze from being drunk and asleep. He gathered his things, put on his pants, and stumbled to Jeronica's room. I slept good that night, even if I didn't get any money, The first experience of a true orgasm was enough to tell him thank you.

The next day before they left we exchanged numbers. We began to talk on a constant basis, he would come up and see me almost every weekend, him and his cousin Derrick. They would take us out to eat every night, Damari was buying me clothes and anything else I needed. Soon it seemed as if they were living with us. They would come down and stay for a whole week with us in our rooms. Shani and I didn't care because they paid for anything we wanted. I started to get curious about their source of income – Lord knows I didn't want to deal with the thug life anymore.

"Damari," I questioned during a phone conversation, "was-sup with your money situation, what do you do?"

"I work with my daddy, he owns a cleaning business, we clean office buildings and daycares, soon he will pass the business on to me and I will be running everything."

I felt like that was acceptable so I didn't mind him spending his money. I had saved up enough money to get a little raggedy car so I could drive back and forth to get my baby. She was my motivation for living.

Things were still crazy at home and getting worse. Towards the end of my sophomore year my dad started to feel like he needed my mom back, he would call her frequently. "Celine, I want my family back together, I want us all under the same roof."

"Are you ready to do what it takes?" she asked.

"Yes, I love you."

"I love you, too."

So now the decision was made that my mom, dad, and brother were all going to be living together in Maryland...five hours away from where I was. During a phone conversation with my mom she broke the news to me. "Celeste, your dad and brother are moving to Maryland with me and we don't think it's appropriate to move Ashley with us."

35

I paused to get my thoughts together. Now it's about to be my junior year, I would rather stay on campus or in campus housing as long as possible, I wasn't ready to be that grown up.

"CELESTE! Are you there?" My mom called.

"Yes, uh okay, well I guess I gotta do what I gotta do." So I had to get an apartment to keep my baby. Aside from my mom's warning, my dad made it clear to me that he was not taking Ashley with him and I made it clear to him that I didn't want him to. I had to do what I had to do, so I went out and got a job, I applied for daycare assistance, food stamps, Medicaid and section 8. I was a student and I needed to survive so I had to rely on any assistance I could get. I was granted daycare assistance, food stamps and Medicaid.

Jeronica was looking to get an apartment too so we decided to move in together, May 2001. Damari would buy me whatever I wanted and take me where ever I wanted. He gave me the money to put the deposit down on my apartment and moved all of my things from the dorm. He and Derrick got jobs working for a delivery company. Jeronica didn't go out much, so between her and Damari they took care of Ashley while I worked or went to class. Soon I got her into a daycare. Life was running smooth. My parents were 5 hours away so the distance was separating for us. My mom and I stayed in contact constantly, I hardly ever spoke to my dad, and my little brother was growing up and doing his own thing. My mom did say that things were going better, my dad was off drugs and his smoking and drinking were cut back. I told her about Damari and the things he had done for me, I liked him a lot.

I started to notice that Damari and Derrick were staying at our house more and more. First they would stay a couple of days then go home, then a couple of days turned into a couple of weeks, and I was getting curious. Finally, they got their own apartment. Life was good. Jeronica and I took turns cooking every night and we would invite them over to eat. As Jeronica, Ashley, and I were about to eat dinner one night when the door bell rang. I got up from our dark burgandyish glass table with black chairs to match. The table was in between the door and the kitchen. Jeronica was putting the food on the table and I was opening the door. "Hey!" I screamed as always to greet Damari and Derrick.

Ashley was sitting in her blue highchair with the white plastic seat cover yelling "Mari and Rick, Mari and Rick!" as she is making this constant bumping noise kicking the chair with her heels. When I looked at their faces they weren't so happy to see us.

"What's wrong wich y'all!" Jeronica yelled curiously. She was from Beauregard, AL, the same place Shani was from, it was very country.

"I lost my apartment," grunted Damari.

"Yo apartment, nigga, that was our apartment and that nigga lost OUR apartment" Derrick yelled in anger.

"WHAT!" is all that could come out of my mouth.

"Dumbass here hasn't paid the rent in three months," explained Derrick as he pushed Damari to the couch. The couch and the love seat made an "L" shape and determined where the dining area stopped and the living room began. The shine from Jeronica's 52-inch TV on Damari's face didn't phase him as he laid there wishing he was invisible. "He drunk, look at him!" Derrick screamed as he stormed out the front door. I had no idea where he was going, he didn't have a car and we were living on the far side of town out by the airport. Anytime somebody says they live by the airport in any city you know it had to be far away from everything.

Inside the house we carried out our night as usual, we ate, I gave Ashley a bath and put her to bed. The next morning it was as if Damari and Derrick were our new roommates. They had nowhere to go so we took them in. Damari and I were falling in love or so I thought. We were having lots of sex. Long, hard, passionate sex. He had a penis that didn't miss a spot and he knew exactly how to work it. One night while Jeronica and Ashley were gone over to Shani's for dinner, Damari and I were watching TV at the house.

"What do you want to eat, babe?" I asked as I gave him a soft pop in the back of the head. Giggling and not paying attention he jumped on top of me and started to tickle me. "STOPPIT BOY, you are so silly!!!!" I can barely talk with his tickle affecting my motion and speech.

Slowing down the mood, he started kissing me slowly from my forehead down to my lips, to my neck, then my chest, to each breast, slipping his hand under my white wife beater, which was my common house attire along with my favorite Spongebob night shorts. Soon Spongebob was face down on the floor and he was kissing where Spongebob once laid his head. He was not one to go down on me. As a matter of fact, he hadn't since the first time we met. So I am getting excited anticipating what he is about to do, using the palm of his hands upon my thighs to push my legs open and up towards his ears, diving mouth first into my private area.

Things started out smooth, until I felt his teeth. First I felt them lightly. "Huh!" I groaned. I think he thought it was a good groan so he started going faster. It was going smooth again, then "Huh, huh." Now I was thinking what the hell is he doing and how do I stop him from doing it. Slowly I grabbed his ears and began pulling him up. "Come on baby, let me feel it."

Relieved from pain, I am adding sounds and groans to express how much I want to feel it as he pulled his pants down. He flipped me over and put it in all in one motion. "AH, AH!" This was more like it and I wasn't faking this time. Suddenly, this had become my favorite position as he thrusted harder.

Smack, smack! Never had that happen before, he was

smacking my ass and I liked it, so I throw it back harder. He grabbed my hair and pulled my head towards him, "Cum with me baby, cum with me," he whispered. It was crazy because him pulling my hair was exciting me more.

"Yes, Yes!" I came and he came shortly after, laying in sweaty bliss. Everything was all good, not even considering the fact that we didn't use a condom. Weeks were passing by and Damari had made himself at home. I started to see a different side of him. Every Wednesday night he would go to "Big Wig's." I have no idea why it was called that but it was a popular bar in Tuskegee. On Wednesdays they would have 20 cent wings and buy-one-get-one-free beers from tap. He had to be there every Wednesday, he would drink until he either ran out of money or the bar shut down. Coming home at 1:00 a.m., slamming the door, "CELESTE! CELESTE!" he yells in a drunken voice. Stumbling to the bathroom, he stands and looks in the mirror calling me.

"What!" I whisper standing at the bathroom door, "Don't wake Ashley, she is sleeping and so is Jeronica."

"I love you gul, I love you," he says drunk and trying to hug me.

"You stink, Damari, I am going back to bed."

He would often sleep right there on the bathroom floor. Week after week the same thing, him coming in stumbling and loud, screaming my name and saying how much he loves me. I was getting fed up with his behavior. It was going on three months straight I had been going through this with him week after week. I decided Wednesday August 22, 2001 that I was going to end this thing. But that morning I woke up sick, feeling nauseated. It woke me up about 9 a.m. so I ran to the bathroom, I knew it! I knew it! Crying and yelling, "Damari!"

Running to the bathroom door, "Wassup babe!"

"I think I am pregnant," holding my head down in tears. He helped me up from the bathroom floor beside the toilet where

I had thrown up. We went to get a test and sure enough it was positive. The summer was over and junior year was starting. I want my baby but I don't want Damari. I questioned myself all weekend.

That night he went out to the bar as usual, this time he came home yelling something different, "I am having a baby! My first baby!" I turned over, put the cover over my head, and went back to sleep.

Over the weekend I questioned myself constantly, "What are you going to do, Celeste? Can you continue to be with a drunk? What about Ashley? What about your unborn child? How will you be a single mother of two?" Here I was praying, "Lord, it's me, I need your help, you know my situation, I need your help."

Sunday night, one of my aunts on my mother's side called me. She and I didn't talk much but love was always understood in my mom's family. "Hello, hey Auntie!"

"Hey Celeste, I don't have but a second because I am on my way to prayer service but the Lord told me to tell you that it's time for you to get back into the fold, now you pray on that and I will talk to you later, love ya, bye."

Sitting with my mouth open, "Bye bye, Auntie." The Lord heard me – I knew what I had to do. "Damari!" I called him from my room to the living room. "Yo"

"ah we need to talk."

"Okay, wassup?

Well, I have been thinking and I am getting ready to get back into church and God and I am going to take a vow of celibacy from now on."

"What! Why! But you are pregnant, that's the best time to do it."

"Well, I am not going to do it anymore."

"So what about me?"

"Yes, and that too. I am tired of your drinking and coming

home all times of night screaming my name, I think it's time you go back to your mom's house.

"Huh? Where is all of this coming from? What is going on? Are you seeing somebody else?"

"No, I am not, I just told you I am getting back into God, seeking the Lord. I had been praying for some things and I got my answer."

"The answer is that you need to break up with me as soon as you find out you're pregnant?"

"No, the answer is I need you to get yourself together if we are going to be together and until then no sex and you need to consider moving back home with your mom and dad."

His parents were faithful Christians; his dad was the pastor of his own church. Very nice people, and he took advantage of them.

He and his father had the same name and he would use his dad's name to get credit cards, run the tab up to thousands of dollars and not even let his dad know. I didn't understand, because they would give him anything that he wanted.

"So, what now?" he asked to conclude this conversation.

"Honestly, I don't know Damari, I know that I can't spend another month with you getting drunk every week. I know I am not having sex anymore."

"Ok, then I guess I am going to have to go back home," he says sadly as he exits the room with his head low.

I exhaled for a moment, satisfied with my decision, and I really felt good about just being alone for a little while. Focusing on God and school. That night I took a vow of celibacy. Damari stayed supportive of me and my daughter. He was so excited the day we found out we were having a boy. I was excited but disappointed. I have a daughter and a son on the way but no man to share this with. The American way teaches us that a married couple with a son and a daughter is the perfect family. Well, I was missing the perfect husband to complete the equation.

"Yeah, you need to marry her," pushed Damari's parents. His sister would pull me to the side and say, "Don't you get married because of a baby, you don't have to marry him." Damari had three older siblings, two sisters and a brother who all lived in Phoenix City, AL. They were very nice people and looked out for me like I was their sister.

I started school and walking around campus with a big belly was hard, but I was more focused than ever. April 25, 2002 my son was born, Joshua Damari Artet. Artet was Damari's last name; he refused to sign the birth certificate if I did not give him his last name. We argued about it a whole day while I was in the hospital until I finally gave up. I didn't want my kids to have different last names. His argument was that a man will carry their last name and a woman will drop hers when she marries. Whatever...I agreed.

Our lease was up in May. Damari was back and forth from Tuskegee to his hometown helping his dad run the family business. They had a cleaning service where they cleaned office buildings. It was pretty profitable...he provided for me and my kids. He moved my entire apartment by himself. I was moving to an apartment closer to school, as a matter of fact, right around the corner from school. It was in walking distance. There was also a daycare in walking distance. It was perfect, a two bedroom one and a half bath townhouse.

I was in the home stretch of my college career and feeling great. The last two years of college is when you really take classes only pertaining to your major, so I was building tighter relationships with people in my major. Damari was always trying to get back with me, but I wasn't having it. The situation was the same between him and my ex-boyfriend I thought that they were people I could be with the rest of my life but when it all falls down they were nowhere near what I really wanted. The question is...did I really know what I wanted?

42

Here I was two kids, not married and no promising relationship, but I was still praying. I was practicing celibacy and getting back into God.

About a month after I moved, Derrick and Jeronica decided to do the roommate thing and moved like one door down from me. There were only four townhouses there, I lived in the second one and they lived in the fourth one. They kept telling me that they were just roommates but I was convinced it was just a little bit more than that. I used that summer as time to gain a focus. I wanted a good life for my children but I had messed up so much already, my kids had two separate fathers, and neither one of them were around or worth much in their lives. One thing I decided was that I would pray for guidance and make the best out of life. Senior year will begin in another month.

CHAPTER 2.

Meet Mitchell

Panting and almost out of breath, running through the woods pushing tree branches out of his face to get through the path faster. "I gotta run, I gotta keep going, I gotta get to my..." the thoughts raced in the mind of Mitchell Austin, 13 years old, running away from the grave site where his father, Mitchell Sr., also know as Mitch, was being buried. His mother, Mrs. Diana Austin, staring through glossy eyes, filled with tears, into the 6 foot deep resting place of a man whom she loved dearly. She didn't feel the need to run after Mitchell being that she knew he couldn't bear the pain and there was only one place the path he ran to could take him, Idle Hour Park a.k.a. Moon Lake Park. The path was a path traveled many times by Mitchell and his dad. During the burial all Mitchell could re-member is how he and his dad walked through that graveyard all the time to reach the path to the park.

Mrs. Diana, also known as Mrs. Di, stood 6 foot tall, brown skinned, short haircut and lots of makeup. She was known in the neighborhood because she fed anybody who was hungry. She had a heart of gold when she wanted to but an attitude from hell if you rubbed her the wrong way. Gripping tightly to her leg was Randy, Mitchell's younger brother. He couldn't really understand being that he was about 5 years younger that Mitchell. All he knew was that his daddy would no longer be around.

"Ashes to ashes and dust to dust, let us pray," the preacher recited as he completed the burial site ritual. As Mrs. Di bowed her head to pray, she remembered Mitch and how good of a father he was. For some reason out of nowhere all the bad thoughts started to rush in also. Mitch was no saint, by the time he died he and Mrs. Di were no longer together. When they were in a relationship she tried her best to stay there, Mitch loved her with all of his heart but could not let go of his craving for women. One woman was never enough for him.

She had been patient with him and his cheating behavior. Women would approach her and try to start a fight. She never minded fighting the adversity of women she thought were jealous of her because she had Mitch. Realization hit when she found that she was fighting the wrong battle. The battle wasn't between her and the angry women – it was between her emotions for Mitch and her conscience guiding her to let go of the hurt and pain. Guiding her to free herself. As these thoughts crossed Mrs. Di's mind briefly, she felt she wiped away all bad memories with paying her respects. He was a great father and a good man when he wanted to be.

Lifting her eyes and walking to the casket to lay her final rose upon it, she whispered, "I always regretted the fact that we didn't make it, over time I realize that it wasn't that I didn't make you the one I loved, but you couldn't find it in your heart to make me the one you loved, rest in peace, Mitch." Kissing the rose she walked away, scared. Not scared of being without him in her life, but scared of him not being in the lives of Mitchell and Randy. About an hour later, she took a trip over to Moon Lake Park to find Mitchell sitting under one of the big oak trees. She didn't feel the need to speak but went and sat beside him.

"Every time we came to this park we did the same things," Mitchell began. "First the swings, then the merry-go-round, then we would race to this very oak tree and sit here for hours. It's funny 'cuz when I think about it, doing the same thing over and over again at the same place seems kind of stupid, but now that I can't do it with him now, it all makes perfect sense."

Kissing him on his forehead Mrs. Di got up, grabbed Mitchell's hand to help him up but she grabbed more than his hand. "What's that in your hand?" she inquired.

"It's my daddy's necklace, the golden cross he always wore. I took it from his dresser because I thought it would have been cool to wear it to school. I was going to give it back to him, but now he is gone."

Mrs. Di then took the necklace from his hand and placed it around his neck. With a smile of great love and understanding, she said, "Now you can wear this just like your dad did, and you can pass it to your son. It will bring you lots of great luck."

Mitchell smiled with assurance as they exited the park and went home. Now life was something different, it was about living, it was about being privileged to see another day.

Mrs. Di dedicated her life to making sure that those boys had everything they wanted. If they wanted any type of material things she got it, hoping to unconsciously substitute material happiness for the pain they had suffered by losing their father. She had no idea how to teach them to be men, and often found herself asking, "What was being all about a man anyway?" That's a hard question for a woman to answer.

At this time Mitchell was a short, dark skinned pudgy kid, but he had really long arms. Since Mrs. Di's blood line was known for being tall, it was expected that Mitchell would not be a little fat kid all his life, and indeed he wasn't. As Mitchell grew older he became very tall and his interest in sports started to grow. He was spoiled. Even though his mom couldn't afford it, he would ask for the newest Jordan's to come out and she got them as soon as the stores opened. She would work two jobs just to get her boys the material things they needed, until one day she came across a couple of boosters. The type of people who would do just about anything for money or drugs, she made these people her acquaintances to ease the strain of spending money on clothes and shoes. From then on everything they had was from a hook-up, they appeared to be rich to people who knew them but Mrs. Di would keep a couple of crack-head friends around to boost for her. Sometimes she would sell the clothes they stole for her and make money off of it for herself. When Mitchell became interested in football she sent him to the best football camps she could find. Football was his favorite sport and with all the training she paid for he had become very good at it. Randy grew up alongside Mitchell but they were so far apart in age that Mitchell was dreaming a whole lot bigger than Randy.

"I am going to be a football star!" Mitchell proclaimed to Randy one morning while getting ready for school.

"No you ain't, you just my brother, I can play betta than you," Randy rebutted.

"No you can't!"

"Yes I can!"

"No you can't!"

"BOYS!" Mrs. Di calls, "Stop all of that yelling and get ya asses ready for school!"

"Yes Mam!" they simultaneously yelled.

Mitchell was in 10th grade now learning how to be a big boy, learning about girls. All his friends from the neighborhood were growing up, too. In the hallway one day, Mitchell passes a flyer on the wall. "Football Tryouts, Wednesday at 3pm" he read out loud to his best friend Corn.

"Shut up nigga, you can't play no football!" Corneilus was

about half Mitchell's height who by this time is about 6 foot. Corneilus was the most trash talking short fat brown-skinned dude in school; they called him "Corn" for short.

"Watch me!" Mitchell said as he winked at Corn. Wednesday came and Mitchell tried out. The coach didn't even wait until the next day to post Mitchell's name. He pulled him to the side after tryouts and told him that he had definitely made the team.

Mitchell's life was changed. He became the football star of his city, Phoenix City, AL, Girls were flocking to Mitchell left and right, he was very popular and carried his team to the finals his junior year. They lost by a field goal in the last few seconds of the game but this was only fuel to Mitchell's fire for what he would do the next year. His mom bought him an old-school Cutlass Supreme, he got the windows tinted and put some Five-Star rims on it the week after he got it.

Life was good according to Mitchell and it got even better. Senior year he took the team back to the finals. At this point the scouts have been following him and scoping him out to recruit him for college. The day of the game came. Mitchell was so anxious all day, he could hardly eat or sit still. Up until this point things had been cool with his love life. He had a girl-friend who he always referred to as Honey because of her light brown skin, 5'9, very light brown skinned, like the color of brown sugar, very slim athletic build of Spanish decent, long dark brown silky hair that stretched to the center of her back, a beautiful girl. He called her Honey so much that even his family called her that. He loved her very much, she was his high school sweetheart, everyone in school knew that was his girl. She was at every game wearing a jersey she had specially made with his number on it. However, since he was so popular he had many girls who wanted to get at him. He called himself having one main girl and then a couple of girls on the side.

48

It was a win-win situation up until he met Keila, 5'6, long hair, coke bottle shaped, dark brown skin. She was of Haitian descent and attended a different high school from the one Mitchell and Honey attended, but she knew that Honey was his girlfriend. In her eyes she felt that she could change that. She also felt that, regardless of the fact that he had a girl-friend, because he was so cute and popular she felt special because she could get his attention.

The day of the final football game that would rank his team as the number 1 high school football team in AL, Mitchell decided he wanted to chill with his main girl Honey, so he planned a special picnic for them at Moon Lake Park under his special oak tree. Arriving at the park around 3 p.m. that afternoon, the only thing on his mind was showing his girl some love and winning the football game.

Keila had been asking Mitchell to see her before the game but he never gave her a definite answer. Keila paced around her room waiting for Mitchell to call. 3 p.m. passed, 4 p.m. passed. "Mitchell, I am waiting, the game starts at 6," she left on his home voicemail about six times. 4:45 p.m. rolled around and Keila hadn't heard from Mitchell. She was now furious and decided to drive over to his mom's house. As Keila pulled up so did Mitchell and Honey laughing and talking about their day at the park.

"Oh, hell no!" Keila yelled to gain their attention. "Who is this bitch?"

Mitchell turned around in total shock and yelled, "What are you doing here?"

Honey was clearly not the adverse type because she broke down and cried, "Mitchell, what is this, who is this, how is this?"

"Look, it's almost 5:30 p.m.. I gotta get ready to go to the game."

"You ain't going nowhere, nigga!" Keila yelled, as she

blocked Mitchell from getting in the house to get ready.

"Yes, I am!" Mitchell yelled back as he pushed Keila to the ground. The only thing on Mitchell's mind was the game. He figured he would deal with this drama later.

Honey followed him into his room. "Mitchell talk to me, why, what, who? I am confused," she cries.

"Look, we will talk about it after the game!"

"After the game? That's all you want to do is go to this stupid game, when you got some girl calling me a bitch."

"Look, Honey, I will talk to you after the game."

Keila was pacing around outside waiting for him to come out. Mitchell hurried to get dressed and out to his car when Keila threw a brick into his windshield.

"BITCH!!!" Mitchell screamed, but time was of the essence so he had no time to dwell on it. He backed out of his driveway and into the street.

"Mitchell, wait!!" Honey screamed and she ran out into the street to get his attention but Mitchell didn't see her and pressed the gas.

"AAAHHH!" Keila yelled.

Mitchell hit Honey by mistake. Getting out of the car he held his head screaming, "NO, NO!!! Go get help, call 911!" he called to Keila.

At the game Mitchell's family and fans were awaiting his arrival. Honey was running out to the car to give Mitchell his dad's cross that he always wore. He had expressed to her how much it meant to him and that it gave him good luck – he never played without it. With the pressure of getting to the game on time and two girls screaming in his ear he had forgotten that he had even taken the necklace off. The coach even put the game off 10 minutes to wait for his arrival, but the game had to go on. Mrs. Di was sitting in the audience confused; she knew that Mitchell was supposed to be on his way. She figured he may have been running late until she received a phone call.

"Ma."

"Mitchell where are you? The scouts are looking."

Mitchell explained what happened and Mrs. Di was stiff with shock. The night was filled with devastation. The team lost the game, Mitchell didn't get to play in the championship game in front of the scouts, Keila caught a charge for the brick in the window, and the worst thing of all, a nosy nurse spread the word that Mitchell had hit a girl with his car. The newspaper took the story and made him out to be a monster. When the scouts found out about the incident they were no longer interested.

Finishing senior year was hard for Mitchell. Honey turned out to be okay – the only thing damaged was her trust in Mitchell. She loved him very much and she thought he loved her. They remained friends and that summer she moved to New York to go to college and never spoke to Mitchell again. After the incident Mitchell broke it off with Keila, hoping to get back in good standing with Honey.

Keila warned, "Mitchell, I hate you, may your days be easy but your relationships hard."

He thought she was crazy. "Whatever, bitch, don't call me anymore, there is no such thing as Haitian voodoo," he responded in a nonchalant tone.

"That's what you think. Mark my words...you will never have a successful relationship!" she yelled as she slammed the phone down.

At this point Mitchell didn't care. He felt like his life was ruined. He coach had always advocated college so he figured he had to go. Mitchell's friends were going to a college close by in Tuskegee, AL at Tuskegee University. Mitchell made the decision to follow his friends and try to start his life with football over again.

CHAPTER 3.

Meet Trinity

"Lord, if my dad is out there, let him come to my birthday party, let him show up and bring me a pretty pink present with something nice inside, please Lord, let him come, amen." A little girl completes her nightly prayer with faith that the father she had never known will come to her 16th birthday tomorrow. Still very child-like she was struggling to grasp the feel of growing up. Trinity Westbrook never really had a father figure in her life. Her dad left her mom, Jessica, when she was about 5. She had vague memories of him and never quite understood why he never came back home, but she held on to knowing his name, Mathew Westbrook. Replaying the mental picture of his loving smile had become a daily routine. Her mother felt she should have been over it by now but at age 16 she often reminisced about being Daddy's little girl.

Trinity was so young when he left them that her mother's reality was not the same as hers. Jessica knew Mathew as a drunken cigarette smoking bum. He could never keep a decent job; Jessica struggled to keep the house running. While grocery shopping one day she met an older man.

"Excuse me miss, what's your name?" Standing in the vegetable section hearing this voice behind her, Jessica hesitated to look back. The only reason she visited the grocery store that night was to get away from home.

Slowly turning to her right to get a full glance at this man, she paused from picking out the good yellow onion she needed for dinner that night and responded by saying, "Jessica, why?"

"Just wanted the opportunity to speak to a beautiful lady like you, I am Kennedy."

Jessica observed that he was a very handsome but older man. He had a medium build, brown skin, close curly haircut, he was about her height 5'9 which was not what she wanted. But hey, she was in a relationship anyway; this was not going to be serious, just a little fun on the side. She was unhappy with her relationship which she had run to the grocery store to get away from. Now she met Kennedy, some man who appeared out of nowhere.

From that day on, Jessica lost the attention that she was paying to Mathew and his drunkenness and found herself out of the house every time she could find a way. Trinity loved to stay at home with her dad whether he was drunk or not. It didn't matter to her...he was her daddy and that's all that mattered. A month later, Jessica was running out of lies to tell to get out of the house.

"Where are you going all dressed up?" Mathew asked as he caught Jessica on her way out the door.

"Uh, remember I told you uh, Trinity has to go to something at her elementary school tonight, Trinity! Let's go, baby, get your shoes."

"Well, I wanna go too, that's my baby."

"Nah uh, you have already had two beers and it's already time to go, let's go baby!" Jessica yelled as she pushed Trinity out of the door. Using Trinity as an excuse was not her intention, but it was done. She was meeting her newfound love, Kennedy, in a nearby park, Moon Lake Park, a very popular park in Phoenix City where they lived. She figured that Trinity could run and play while she sat and talked to him.

"Hi there, little lady," Kennedy said to Trinity.

"Hi Mister," she responded in her little 5 year old voice.

"Uh, go play baby," Jessica urged. Trinity ran off to play. She played with all the other kids on the playground with no idea of what was going on. As she was sliding down the slide she glanced over to gain a smile of approval from her mom but she saw her mom kissing the "mister." She was confused but continued to play until her mom called for her. After about an hour and a half the park was becoming empty and it was getting dark.

"TRINITY!" Jessica called. Trinity ran over to her mother panting and out of breath. She knew it was time to go.

"See ya later, little lady," Kennedy said as he handed her a lollipop.

Trinity smiled and said, "Thank you Mister, bye bye."

Jessica was floating on air as she always did after seeing Kennedy. Arriving home that night, Jessica sneaked in past drunken Mathew laid back snoring on the couch. She got Trinity ready for bed, but Trinity just couldn't finish her lollipop before lying down. She didn't want to lie down and eat it so she ran to the living room. "Daddy, daddy, look I have a lollipop."

Still halfway drunk and passed out of the couch, he opens his eyes to see that she does have a lollipop. "Oh baby, well you do, don't you?" he grunted out of his sleep.

"Yeah and I got it from a nice Mister."

"A nice Mister? Where was the nice Mister?"

"At the park with Mommy. You know him, Daddy, you gotta know him because she kissed him like she kiss you."

Sitting up straight in the chair from shock Mathew was suddenly sober. He had been suspicious for a while. "Well, that's enough lollipop baby, it's time to go to bed. Where is

Mommy?"

"She is in the shower."

But Jessica was no longer in the shower. She was putting on her night clothes when she overheard this conversation between Trinity and Mathew. She paced around the bedroom trying to figure out what would happen next.

After taking the lollipop away from Trinity and tucking her in the bed, Mathew headed for the bedroom. "I knew it bitch!" he yelled while bringing his right hand down across her left cheek. Jessica screamed and screamed while Mathew beat the shit out of her for at least ten minutes.

He would have continued but Trinity walked in screaming, "DADDY, DADDY!!" Coming to reality from his little girl's scream, Mathew walked out of the room, stormed out of the house, and never came back. That night was the last night Trinity saw her dad. Jessica sent her back to bed and never even tried to explain or comfort her. Trinity wasn't Daddy's little girl at all, according to Jessica.

"If he loved you he would have never left you," she would explain to Trinity when she would cry at the age of 9 from wanting her daddy back. Jessica would put Trinity in every beauty pageant she could get her in.

Trinity wasn't the prettiest little girl but she had a nice fit shape, which caused any outfit to look good on her. She was dark skinned with very long dark hair. Trinity's perception of her pageant life was different: all the other little girls in the pageant had their fathers in the audience, cheering them on, but when she looked out at the faces in the crowd she knew her father's face was not one that she would see.

When Trinity turned 10 Jessica let the man that Trinity knew as "Mister" move in with them. She figured that Trinity was old enough now to know and accept that her dad was never coming back. Whether she did or not was not really a concern of Jessica's. Her relationship with Matthew was so bad that she was just happy to have a man in her life who made her feel good. Kennedy was unable to have children because of a vasectomy he had two years prior to meeting her, so she adopted a little boy. This was the only sibling Trinity knew. Later in life she found out that she had lots of sisters and brothers by her father that she never had a chance to connect with because she had no contact with her father.

Her mom had planned a beautiful sweet 16 party for her. Now, overhearing her prayer for her father to come, Jessica was disappointed. She felt as if she had done a great job raising Trinity. "Why did she still want to know that no good father of hers?" she complained to Trinity's adopted brother.

The birthday party came and went but Trinity's father never showed up. She was very disappointed by this. When she blew out the candles she secretly wished to meet him again one day. After that day she decided to go on an extensive search for this man she wanted to know as her dad. Her mom would not give her much info at first but she gave in after Trinity cried to her night after night about it.

Her mom finally decided to help her find him. It took her about two years to track him down. By her junior year in high school she finally had some positive info. Using several people-finder services and paying about two thousand dollars of her money her mother took from Kennedy, she had an address, which was surprisingly right around the corner from her high school. She was too afraid to go to the house so she procrastinated on actually visiting him. However, just having the address was a feeling of relief for her. At least she knew where he was. As senior year rolls around she was starting to gain a little confidence. She would ride by the house every day and get too nervous to knock on the door.

"Ma, will you go to the house with me?"

"Hell no, fuck him, I don't want to see that bastard," her mother would shout.

"But Ma, please, how will I know if it's really him?" Trinity stomped off to her room crying. Trinity's mom didn't care much for her after her dad left them. She held everything that he had done to her against Trinity. Trinity found herself lost and confused for a while in high school, especially after her sweet 16 disappointment.

After weeks of begging Trinity's mom agreed to go with her to the address she had found in her search. One Monday afternoon they took a ride by the address she was given by one of the agencies that had helped her. As they pulled up to the house.

"Okay, I ain't going to the door witcha!" her mom yelled.

Teary eyed, Trinity stared at the the door of the house through the car window. "Go on!" Startled by her mom's loud voice, she opened the car door, took a deep breath, and marched up to the door with determination. She raised her hand to knock but felt a nervous weak feeling for a second and dropped her hand. Quickly she raised her hand again and knocked on the door as if to try to do it without thinking too much about it.

After about two minutes of staring at the door, finally the door opened. "Hello, can I help you?" a woman asked.

"Yes, I am looking for Mathew Westbrook," Trinity said in a low crackling voice.

"Hold on, baby. MATT!" the lady yelled behind her shoulder but still staring at Trinity. "SOMEBODY AT DA DO FO YA!"

A tall slender dark skinned man approaches the door from behind this woman. "Well, who is it?" he said as he approached the door. Trinity was in awe and could hardly speak. It was like looking in a mirror, he had a slender face shaped like hers, big bright eyes like her, puffy cheeks, she didn't know what to tell him and the lady now standing behind him was making things worse.

"Well, how can I help ya, honey, I am Mathew Westbrook."

"Ah, ah, I am Trinity Westbrook," she stuttered.

For a second the man's eyes grew bigger and brighter. Standing with his mouth open he examined her face. "Trinity?" he whispered in hidden excitement. Peeping around her and into the car she drove up in he saw her mother sitting in the car. His facial expression suddenly changed from excited and bright to grumpy and angry. "Nah, nah, I don't know no Trinity Westbrook," he grunted as he turned to return to the back of the house.

"But wait, wait, I am your dau..." Trinity could not even finish her sentence before he slammed the door in her face. Trinity turned and ran back to the car. Trinity's mother stared at the house and saw Mathew peeking through the blinds at them as Trinity returned to the car. They caught an unforgettable eye contact that symbolized the anger between both of them.

"I told your ass not to come over here, I told you to just leave it alone, I am ya mama and ya daddy," Trinity's mother explained in a mean, insensitive way.

Since then Trinity looked at men differently. She found herself afraid of having a boyfriend. She didn't know if one little thing that she might do would send him away for good. She started to realize how bitter her mom was. None of the guys that Trinity would bring home were good enough, according to Jessica. They all reminded her of Trinity's father. Things were not as great with Kennedy as Jessica had planned. She caught him cheating with one of the secretary's at his job. After seeing her mom cry, Trinity express to her mom that she should leave him alone, "NONSENSE!" Jessica would yell, remember, if you want a man you will have to put up with things to keep him, that's just the way it is baby.

At this point, Trinity was about to graduate from high school. She had every intention of getting out of her mom's house so she applied for any college she could think of. Alabama was all she knew so she didn't want to move too far. She got accepted to Alabama A&M, Alabama State, and Tuskegee University.

"Ma, I think I will go to Alabama A&M," she informed her mom at dinner one night.

"Uh, no you won't, I say you are going to Tuskegee because it's the closest. You can't live too far from me. You can't even take care of yourself, always crying about something."

"But Ma!" Trinity knew Tuskegee University was in Tuskegee, Al, only about an hour from Phoenix City. That was too close to her mom. She wanted to be as far away as she could without leaving Alabama.

"But Ma, nothing, I have to help you make decisions. If I didn't you would still be crying over that no good father of yours."

"May I be excused?" Trinity asked in a very low voice.

"Yes, you may. Throw your plate away on your way outta the dining room."

Holding back the tears, Trinity got up from the table, threw her plate away, and went to her room to cry. Trinity cried until she concluded that even if she was only an hour a way at least she was away from the bitter heart of her mom. That fall she moved onto the campus of Tuskegee University.

CHAPTER 4.

Celeste Meets Mitchell

July 2002, at the basketball gym on our college campus, Tuskegee University, where my friends and I are all juniors, I am introduced to Mitchell Austin, 6'3, 220 pounds of chocolate, he is tall and stalky but not fat at all. I had heard the buzz on him from my girls but this is the first time I have seen him in person, he was a great football player in high school and uses basketball to stay in shape. He is cuter than I thought. I adore the way his tight butt is positioned in his basketball shorts and the way his athletic calf muscles areshaped as he pushes from his toes when shooting the ball.

Walking into the gym with my friend Keisha that day I have no intentions of meeting someone new. "Wassup Keisha," he calls as she walks over to do what we call "dap him up," which is when you make a fist and softly pound it on top of the other person's fist.

"Nothing much." Turning slightly towards me, Keisha introduces us, "Celeste Mitchell, Mitchell Celeste."

He reaches out to shake my hand and I am stunned just looking into his eyes. "Wassup," I stutter, finally sticking out my hand to shake his. He is looking me straight in my eyes as if to look straight through me. Our eyes are locked for a second, then he turns and starts shooting around the goal again. Leaving his presence he has made a mark in my mind just that quick. I go upstairs to work out but he stays on my mind.

Keisha is one of my best friends; we have the same major and we met by having so many classes together. Good people recognize good people. She is about 5'10 brown skinned, she has the prettiest long dark brown hair you have ever seen, an athletic shaped body, not fat, built like a basketball player. She is very into sports and that's how I began coming to the gym. She plays basketball in the gym with the boys. She came from a good home with both parents just like me. However, they were a little more wealthy than my parents. Students who had the opportunity to grow up that way were few and far between so I was glad to meet her. I would go up to the gym with my son who was now about 5 months old and my daughter who was 3, to watch Keisha and her friend Nicole play basketball with the boys. Nicole and I met through Keisha, she was dark skinned about 5'9/5'10, small shape but toned. Nicole also has an athletic build; she always has a mean look on her face but is really cool people.

Some days I go work out and some days I just watch. Mitchell and I just say hi and keep moving. Around October I notice I hadn't seen him in the gym a couple of days so I ask Louis, Mitchell's roommate, where he was. "He has been on a trip to Vegas and will return soon," Louis informs me. Louis had a thing for Keisha. He is about 6' tall brown skinned, laid back, but very playful at times. He and Mitchell played ball together in high school, Tuskegee, AL. There must have been something in the water down there to make us fall for these niggas.

"Well, tell Mitchell I said hello." When I said tell him I said hello, I really meant tell him I said hello but Louis thought otherwise.

That night I go to see Shirley Caesar speak at a church

nearby. Shani asked me to go with her so I said yes, but I was disappointed, once Shirley Caesar started comparing the amount of offering to give to the amount of blessings we would receive. I was nudging Shani to say let's get outta here. Shani agrees, so we gather the children up and head for the door. I find myself getting angry when I cannot exit the parking lot because I am blocked in, sitting in my four door 1989 Blue Honda Accord in the rain. We are parked on a muddy terrain and there is a car parked in front of me and behind me. I am trying to pull up and back to get room to exit through the driveway on the left. I am ready to go but Shani is keeping me cool.

As my frustration is slowly building up my cell phone rings. The voice on the other end is one that had never been there before. "Wassup," echoes a deep sexy voice through the other end of the line. I look at the phone as if it is playing a trick on me. He must have the wrong number. "Who is this?" I answer back

"Mitchell, from the gym, my roommate told me that you said hello."

Now feeling surprised, happy, and jittery, I say, "Uh yeah hey."

Louis grabs the phone from him saying, "Yeah, Celeste, you told me to tell him hello." Mitchell returns to the phone and I am sitting in a state of shock and frustration from not being able to get out of the parking lot. I tell him what is going on and that I will call him back. I immediately call Keisha to yell my excitement in her ear.

Since each one of my friends is paired with one of his friends they knew him better than I did. They brag on how he is the best one out of all of his boys. How he is laid back and works a lot. Mitchell is tall, dark, and handsome...every woman's dream. He has a nice build that is solid but soft like an expensive teddy bear.

62

As soon as I get the chance to return his phone call I do, and we click from day one. Our conversations are stimulating and last for hours. He tells me all about his past and his future goals. "So tell me about you," I say to spark a conversation.

"What do you want to know?" he answers back to throw the ball back into my court.

"Everything."

"Okay, well, I was born and raised in Phoenix City, Alabama. I loved it there, I was a high school football star, very close to an all American but some things happened and I just lost the love for football."

On that note I don't question him about football anymore. "I am sorry to hear that."

"It's cool," he says to comfort my concern. He goes on to explain that he didn't have any kids but had two younger brothers, Thomas and Randy. Thomas was the youngest, 10 years old, full of talent, but wanted to be a bad ass in school. Mitchell expresses that he had far more potential than him and Randy. Thomas is his half brother from his mom's marriage. Randy and Mitchell had the same father, who had passed when Mitchell was in 8th grade, from cancer.

Mitchell mentions his father's death very briefly. "My dad was a good daddy, he would take us for long walks and play with us, and he made sure we had what we needed," he says in a low voice, which signified that this was a touchy subject. "My brother Randy looks just like him."

On a lighter note he quickly switches the conversation over to describing his brother. Randy, as he described him, has a pretty boy attitude. He is 18 and about to graduate from high school. He has a smart mouth and is definitely suffering from "MCS." "MCS?" I question.

"Middle Child Syndrome."

We laugh together and continue talking all night. I share my life story and he shares his. Things are perfect. He is like

63

a piece of my puzzle waiting to be put in place. We complete each other's sentences and are always thinking the same things at the same time. Things are so freaky until one day we are watching TV together at his house and at the same moment we take the decorative pillow from behind us and place it in front of us. It is synchronized like we had planned it. We look at each other like "WHOA!"

Mitchell is perfect for me. I explain to him my celibacy and he is a perfect gentleman about it. He never tries to have sex with me. I tell him how I am deep into the church and I had been celibate for a year and two months, and counting. He respects that. He also accepts the fact that I have two kids and two different baby daddies, one which is never really around and I had to put up for child support earlier that year and one who is around, who cares about both of my kids equally but is not completely over the fact that he and I have nothing going on.

I have very good friends and a cousin named Erica who has come to live with me so a baby sitter is never a problem and I have plenty of support. She is a sophomore and is just staying with me since she recently found out that she is pregnant. I didn't want her to drop out of school and the dorm life was not the life for a pregnant woman.

My townhouse is just big enough for us. When you walk in the front door there is the half bath to your left, then a couple of steps up to the right is the kitchen. Then you enter a small living room which is big enough for my two gray and cream plaid couches, a black glass table, a wooden entertainment center purchased at a yard sale, and my daughter's Barbie 4-wheeler which can't fit into her room. The couch is up against the wall where the steps are, and over the couch is a big cream and gray picture of a vase and flowers, which is outlined with a mirror. Damari's mom got it for me. She would go to auctions all the time and buy things she didn't need. That is how I decorated most of my house.

Mitchell never really says much about my kids. When he sees them he plays with them a little but that's it. Out of sight out of mind. I figure once we get serious he will warm up to them and try to form a relationship with them. I don't want to push him away so I let it slide. We sleep in the bed together numerous times and he never tries anything. This makes me want him more.

Mitchell explains how he wants me to wait until I am ready and he won't force it on me. We are together almost every day. If I'm not in the gym watching him play basketball, I'm at his house. He never really comes to see me as much as I go to see him but I ignore this and hope that the kids won't scare him away.

One night he comes to spend the night with me. My son is about 8 months at this time and starts crying in the middle of the night. When you come up the stairs, the full bath is straight ahead. To the left is my daughter's room. She has bunk beds. The bottom bed is a full bed which is where Erica sleeps. The top is a twin bed, which is Ashley's space. Further left is my room.

My room is very spacious and has a long closet with two great big sliding doors. My son's white crib with the Winnie the Pooh sheets and mobile is across from my full princess-style bed that Mitchell and I are sleeping in. I slowly crawl out of bed to get him as if the crying didn't already wake Mitchell up. The room is about pitch black aside from the little bit of light somehow shining from my daughter's night light into my room.

As I pick Joshua up he is reaching toward Mitchell. Now I am confused. Does he want Mitchell to hold him? This is new. So Mitchell reaches out and takes him into his arms, but he crawls over Mitchell to the table on the side of the bed to get his cup. I lay him back in his crib with his cup and he goes back to sleep.

Feeling uneasy, stupid, and embarrassed, I get back in the bed thinking this man is gonna leave me alone for sure. I toss and turn all night wondering what he is thinking. I prepared myself for failure, but the next day we chill like everything is cool. Nothing changes, he treats me the same, and he still plays with the kids when he sees them. I exhale and start to trust in Mitchell and that's where things get deeper. When I get alone I write about how great this man is making me feel:

Between us there is only love and faithfulness.
If I am out with my friends and he is out with his,
he doesn't worry about what we do
because we always stay true.
I will give him my last dime.
If I didn't have one he would say,
"Here, take mine."
He tells me I'm right when I am wrong,
we never have boring conversations on the phone.
We always say "I love you" before hanging up.
People say God put us together;
maybe we're stuck or it might be just luck.
We are lovers as well as best friends,
whenever you need me you can depend.
You greet me with a hug and a kiss
and you always let me know it's me that you miss.
All of me is yours to keep,
I'm more than enough so there is no need to cheat.
What's mine is yours and yours is mine,
when we're apart I think of you all
the time. My heart is filled with love for you,
by the things you do you show me that yours is too.

CHAPTER 5.

The First Encounter

Mitchell and I eat at a different restaurant almost every day. I work part time at a Starbuck's so we eat Danishes and drink lattes outside on the patio on my lunches. He picks me up from work and we just drive around and look at big houses in the white neighborhoods, comparing them to what we want our house to look like. He is the first guy I have dated that has everything in his personality I want, plus looks. However, he does have a really bad acne problem that just won't go away. I used to joke with him about being a Proactive spokesperson, but the bumps never bothered me. He is very self conscious about it, but when you like someone you tend to overlook the things that make him or her insecure.

As Mitchell and I continue dating, about three months later we end up in the same club one night. I walk in, I see Mitchell, give him a big hug, order me a Blue Motorcycle from the bar even though I am already tipsy because my friends and I were drinking before we got there. I throw the bartender a $20 bill; my drink is $8. As I leave her a $5 tip, I turn to notice Mitchell's ex-girlfriend trying to talk to him. Putting my large regular size glass up to my mouth, I try to hide the fact that my eyes are cutting to the right to look at how he is ignoring her. He gives her an "I don't want to talk about it" light push of her hand off his shoulder as he grabs his drink from the bartender and walks away from her.

She doesn't know who I am but he had told me all about her. Her name is Trinity Westbrook, her people were from Louisiana, where people were known for putting roots on people. She doesn't have a pretty face but has a nice petite shape. She has hopes of being a model but knows she can't cut it as high fashion because she's too short. She is currently modeling for a local campus-modeling group and is pursuing a degree in fashion design. Realistically speaking, she is a dummy. What will she do with a fashion design degree in Alabama?

She and Mitchell were together for a year and had been broken up for about a year when he met me. Mitchell mentioned that while they were broken up they were still doing the same things as when they were together, so when he decided to try and leave her alone she didn't like it at all.

In a previous conversation about how Mitchell was such a good guy, Keisha explained that she thought he had a crazy ex-girlfriend but crazy was too friendly a word to use for this girl. Mitchell also told me how she tried to kill herself over him by taking a bunch of pills, because he told her that it was over. She told him that if she couldn't have him she didn't want to live. He was like, "Whatever!" and brushed it off, but that night she swallowed a whole bottle of her roommate's prescription sleeping pills. Her roommate came in and found her on the floor foaming at the mouth, they rushed her to the hospital, she was in a coma for two days and the dumb-ass girl lived.

Her mother blamed Mitchell and ever since that day his family has had a bad taste in their mouth for Trinity. Mitchell was the first person that she felt really loved her. She would try and cling to her mom but she didn't have much success with that. Her mom would treat the adopted son better than she would treat her. Mitchell was also the first man she had sex with, so she was definitely strung out over him.

Now all of this is in the back of my mind as I observe the club scene. After Mitchell walks away she glances over at me with a snarling squench-eyed look. I know that she is about to approach me so I walk back over to my friends to prepare myself. However, little do I know this night is the first of many nights of drama to come.

I brush that incident off even though he walks out after her as if he needed to explain why he just played her face in front of me. I spend the night trying to make sure I am seeing this thing clearly. Ex-girl approaches me saying she is his girl and asking me crazy questions, then approaches him in front of me. He denies her, then walks out after her. Something is not adding up.

The next day we spend the whole day at the park talking about Trinity and her place in his life. "So what is up with her approaching me saying all of this then you leave out of the club after her, I don't get it," I question him.

"Nothing is up, we are just cool, she is mad because I won't be with her. We are good friends, we have been through a lot together. I walked out after her because I don't like to burn bridges. I didn't apologize, I just confirmed what I said in front of you and told her to stop approaching people I date."

"So this has happened more than once."

"Yes, I have had girls that were just my friends and I was having sex with them but she didn't know that. She would see me talking to them at the club or school events and later on she would approach them asking them if they are dating me or having sex with me. One of the girls almost whipped her ass, " he chuckles. "She is crazy in a sense but we are just friends, I promise you." Then he leans in to kiss me and I am mad so I don't want to but I can't resist.

69

We spend the next two hours sitting on the grass in the park chatting about where we want our life to go. He has dreams of owning his own computer company and getting as big as Bill Gates someday, and I share my dreams of becoming a great writer. I used to write poems in my spare time and on days that he and I go to the park I read them to him. That is something I have never done. All through high school I wrote but I never read them or let anyone read them.

Mitchell and I grow closer. Seeing each other every day is not enough for us. At this time he is working for a local computer company as a graphic artist. He has free time during the day while designing so we talk on the phone as much as possible. After he gets off work we go out to eat at our favorite restaurant called Anderson's Bar and Grill. Sometimes his friends and their girlfriends join us for dinner and drinks.

As of now it's been about 6 months and we have not had sex. We are on another level where sex is not a big issue and I love it. After going out one night we retire at his house. It was understood that if we ended up there I was staying the night. He has the most comfortable bed, queen size; the comforter is a really light yellow to beige color with black Chinese writing all over it. He has the bed skirt to match with some hint of burgundy stripes, which matches his bathroom set: burgundy decorative towels, shower curtain, and bath mat. His room is always clean, a closet full of clothes, a rack of shoes taller than him with everything from Timberland boots to Cole Hanns.

I am definitely impressed and loving his taste and figuring by the way everything is matching that he has to be a mama's boy. When I walked into his room I can't help but notice the chifforobe to the right with a 32-inch TV sitting on it. Straight ahead is the dresser with a big mirror and a night stand which all match perfectly in a soft-toned wood. Good furniture, clean room, nice shoes, and a big TV, he has got to be the one. I slept in his bed a couple of times before but for some reason I am feeling like this is the night to give it up. He doesn't know I gave myself a pep talk all the way home in the car. "Celeste, this man is the one, look at him, sexy, smelling good, talking to me in a deep voice that is making me wet."

I hold my composure. I haven't had sex in a year and now I find my self about to undress in the car. BUT I hold on till we reach his room. He turns around from closing the door and there I stand already undressed and wearing my soft purple lace bra which snaps in the front and matches with my purple lace boy cut underwear. He stands dumbfounded for a second but starts to kiss me. He asks me if I am sure I am ready repeatedly but is not pausing to check and see.

"Are you sure, I wanna make sure you're ready," he says as he unsnaps the front of my bra and begins to caress my nipples with his tongue...alternating from left nipple to right nipple. I try to remain calm as if I don't wanna slam him on the bed and do this thing all by myself. Then he starts slowly down my chest to my belly. He kisses all the way down to my secret place. He kisses all over it, then down to kiss on each thigh. Slips off my panties and my secret place becomes public information. He slips on some protection and starts back at my breast. I am anticipating a nice thrust of passion any second now.

"Oh my gosh, put it in, stop teasing me!" is what I am shouting in my mind. "Huh, huh," breathing hard, almost panting at this point, and he shoves in a wiener. What I thought was going to be the best sex ever was like taking a ballpark frank and putting it into a hole the size of a spare tire. I laugh to myself but it was okay because I hadn't had sex in forever so the anticipation and the fact that I finally had a man on top of me makes it work.

But I laugh once I get home that morning. I call Keisha, "Girl, guess what!"

71

"Wassup," she replies in a subtle voice as if she is preparing herself for what I am about to say.

"I had sex with Mitchell last night."

If I could see the other side of the phone...I can tell by her voice she sits straight up on her couch and says, "How was it girl?!"

"It was an Oscar Myer weiner child."

"HAHA!!!" she bursts into laughter. "For real girl?"

"YES! but the foreplay was good and I hadn't had sex in forever, I don't know, maybe I will give him another chance."

"Well, what is his ex-girlfriend so crazy about?" she laughs.

"You see how small she is...that's probably about all she can handle," I laugh back.

The next night Mitchell and I have dinner with his barber, Bobby. Bobby is about 5'9 250 pounds, light skinned, light brown eyes, close haircut, and is always joked on in the barbershop because of his weight. He is one of the nicest people I have ever met. He is a comedian...always has something funny to say. He is a little older and more mature than some of Mitchell's friends. He keeps my eyebrows shaped up for free because of Mitchell so I go to the barbershop and laugh at his jokes every other week. We sit and talk about different subjects for hours. When we plan to go out to eat together he says, "Let's go out to eat as a family." I have a great time just being around him.

Mitchell's friends, Tommy, Jesse, Jacob, and Louis, his roommates are all dogs and at the time matched up with one of my friends. Nicole and Jacob who is about 5'11 chocolate skinned, he is a skinny guy but has a nice build, his clothes and shoes are always fresh and he has sexy lips like Memphis Bleek. As a matter of fact, I think he looks a lot like him. There is Kelly and Jesse who is high yellow with the ego of a rich white man and the looks of a mediocre insurance salesman. I had a class with him freshman year and he just always seemed like an ass kisser. Keisha and Louis are messing around also so some nights we both end up staying over at the same time and then leaving and going to class together that morning. I have a key to Mitchell's place so she and I are in the house chilling by ourselves until time for class.

And his last friend Tommy is just out there, 5'7 light skinned, bald headed, he was not ugly but had a wandering eye that could get creepy if you were to have a drunk one night stand and then wake up beside him. He is one of those cool, selfish, no job having, I might need your couch tonight kinda friends. At times we would all meet up and go out to eat and hang out at the gym. They all play basketball, but I have no athletic ability so I work out and watch the girls play with the boys.

After hanging out with everybody one night at Chili's, Mitchell and I decide to go back to his place. I know what he is working with now and I am not a fan of it at this point. So I am not pressed to jump back in the bed with my best underwear and bra on again. This time my panties and bra are not even matching and I think one of my socks has a hole in it, but what the hell, it will be dark and after one good feeling he will be asleep. But to my surprise when we hit the bed this time, things are different. Everything starts off the same...slow and passionate. As always, the foreplay is enough to make me cum. He loves caressing the nipples and I'm not going to stop him. He likes to take it slow, he has mastered the art of anticipation. Slowly he begins to thrust but the condom is not working for either of us so he asks if it is okay if he takes it off.

Being that the last person I had sex with was my son's dad and we never used a condom, I don't like using them so I shake my head yeah and he takes it off. I realize that he must have been serious with Trinity if he felt comfortable not using a condom the second time we have sex.

73

But when he takes it off it's like it grew like Pinocchio's nose. This time the thrust is bigger, harder, and deeper, and worth a second try. I have to inhale to take it all in at one time, but once it is in it's a perfect fit. Now I am definitely in love, I feel complete. Good sex, nice guy, no kids, nice job, goals, what more do I need? This sexual escapade ends for the night and I have to leave to get back home. I kiss him and hug him goodnight, well, good morning because it's now about 2 in the morning. I dance down his apartment steps feeling like a crisp $100 bill. As soon as I place my key into the car door I hear a whispering but wondering voice, "Excuse me."

I turn around to see Trinity, standing in what now is a light drizzle in a jean jacket, a white wife beater and some sweats, her hair in a pony tail as if she rushed out of the house to check up on a cheating boyfriend. I walk up towards the steps to listen to what she had to say. "It's 2 in the morning, what do you want?" I ask in an irritated voice.

She begins questioning. "Are you having sex with him? Do you sleep in his bed? Does he take you out to eat?"

Realizing that she is serious, I reply, "Why, will it make a difference if I tell you yes to everything? Would that make you leave me alone? It's none of your business, what the hell is wrong with you, why are you out here? You love this man very much, don't you?" I ask as if I really care.

"Yes," she replies.

I walk away shaking my head and she walks up the stairs and proceeds to knock on the door. I hesitate to pull off to see what is going to happen. To my surprise he opens the door and she walks in. So I cut my car off and storm up the steps to see what is going on. He is opening the door and pushing her out as I walk in.

"What's going on Mitchell?" Trinity asks.

"Look, y'all are not about to start fighting in here so I don't want to hear it." was the first thing to come out of his mouth.

I brush through the door past them both and take my place on the couch. Hushed from disappointment, thinking I can't believe this shit! He walks back into the living room area and sits on a barstool in front of a small bar that you could look over into the kitchen and see the small "L shaped" kitchen with just enough area to get into the fridge and cabinets as well as cook. I am sitting on the couch which is up against the wall which made an "L shape" with the couch which separates the side of the room with the bar and kitchen from the living room area where the TV is. The love seat, couch, and TV all make an incomplete square with a glass table in the middle.

She keeps asking him what's going on and pulls a piece of my hair from his head. I chuckle and she is getting madder by the minute. So when I get my nerves together to say something I ask, "Are you his girlfriend?"

She looks at him and asks, "Am I, Mitchell?"

He stares back at her and shouts, "Are you? Tell her the truth...are you?" Then, in a very nonchalant tone he says, "Look man, I am not going to go through this tonight."

"I don't have time for this!" I shout as I jump up off the couch and storm out the door.

"Celeste, don't go," Mitchell says as he reaches for my arm as I pass by him to get to the door. He misses touching my arm by an inch and I storm out the door. Riding home I replay the night in my head. Who is this girl? Is this really his girl? Is he having sex with her? I get home, turning my key softly and being careful not to wake my cousin and my babies.

I have to go home tonight because my cousin has an early class. My class isn't until 10; I am pursuing a degree in computer science. After school I don't know what I want to do with my life but I know I want to move closer to my mom, dad, and brother. I figure the pay has to be better there than living here in Alabama.

As time goes on I question Mitchell about this girl that won't go away. He says, "She is just mad because I won't be with her, we are just friends, we are cool."

A year passes and she pops up more and more frequently, every week or every other week. Banging at his door all times of the night. Most of the time we are on the phone when it happens or he tells me about it the next day. He tells me how he literally has to pick her up and throw her out of the house.

Running parallel with this is the fact that we are spending every day together...he becomes one of my best friends. I leave my friends to see him; I cancel plans with my friends to see him. We please each other on all levels. It is wonderful.

He introduces me to his family and I introduce him to mine. We are becoming a great part of each other's lives. He is the first guy that I have ever really let around my kids. All the bliss makes me ignore the drama that Trinity is causing. I argue with him every time she pops up and ask him to stop talking to her but he always explains that she is nobody, just a crazy ex-girlfriend, obsessed and mad because he won't be with her. So I trust him, really I have no reason not to. If we are together and she pops up he always tells her to leave us alone and to go home.

I gain a closer relationship to his family by going home with him on holidays when I am not with my kids or family. My son's father and his parents favor my children and take them for weeks at a time during the summer months, which frees up more time for me and Mitchell. People know us, if they see Mitchell they ask where is Celeste. We are always together around his friends and family.

At the beginning of the summer I am at home with my children talking on my home phone, 3-way with my mom and my aunts when my cell phone rings. It's about 1 in the morning and I am wondering who the hell is this? It is Louis asking in a panicked-type voice, "Have you talked to Mitchell?"

"What's wrong?" I ask, concerned. I tell my family I will call them back and return to the conversation with Louis. He says once again, in a hurry this time, "Have you talked to Mitchell?"

By this time, Mitchell is beeping in on my other line. "Hold on, Louis, this is Mitchell right here."

Before I get to say hello good, Mitchell says, "Come get me from downtown."

"Downtown as in your car broke down or as in you're in jail?"

"I am in jail, Celeste, please come get me."

"Okay, I am on my way," I reply as if I am a super hero.

Returning back to Louis on the other line asking, "What happened?"

"Are you going to get him? They won't release him to me because I am drunk."

Being the superwoman I am, I say, "Okay, I am on my way." Not taking into consideration that my car is broken down and Erica was gone home for the summer. With two kids in the bed how in the hell am I going to save the day?

Luckily, Jeronica lived two doors down. I run down to get her and borrow her car, she stays at the house with my kids, she is a good friend indeed. I am racing to the jailhouse thinking, "What the hell is going on?" I get there, talk to the magistrate, and sit in the waiting area. I never understood why it takes so long to get someone out of jail but the wait keeps my mind racing. I call Louis back to question him again but he wouldn't give me any straight answers. "Louis, what happened, what is going on?"

"I have his car, I am going back to the club but don't tell him that."

"WHAT HAPPENED!!"

"I will let him tell you, my battery is going dead on my phone."

Hanging up the phone frustrated I overhear a conversation behind the glass at the magistrate's desk. A conversation between the magistrate and the police. "Name: Trinity Westbrook 2425 Oakwood Place, she says that he busted her door down because she had another man in the house."

"Is he drunk?"

"No."

"Well, let's go ahead and release him."

Now I am furious, confused, frustrated, and I really have no words for him. So I have been sitting downtown in a waiting area to get a man out of jail who busted down another girl's door because she has another man in there. This is the same girl that has been stalking us for the past I don't know how long. I am about to walk out of the waiting area and leave his ass, as they release him. He walks up to me to welcome me with a hug as if we are at a family reunion or something.

"Don't hug me," I say with the stern voice of a mad black woman. "What happened?" I ask.

"Don't hug you? See you always assuming something," he says as if I didn't just get him out of jail.

Now in the car on the way to his house I ask in an aggravated voice, "You knocked her door down? Why did you knock her door down? Because there was another dude in the house?"

"Hell, no! That's not why."

"Why then, Mitchell, why?"

"You don't understand."

"Well, make me!"

"We got into an argument and she said something I didn't like."

"She said something you didn't like!" I am shouting to the top of my gums, "I just got your ass out of jail, Negro...what do you mean she just said you something you didn't like?"

He must think I am Boo Boo the fool. His house is only about 5 minutes from the jail. As we pull up in front of his house I am furious and he is trying to explain. "It was nothing, you know my attitude, she said something that pissed me off and I wanted to finish what I had to say." Just then Louis pulls up with his truck,he leans to kiss me on the cheek and I pull away. "Celeste, please don't act like that, thank you for coming to get me."

I look him in his eyes and tell him, "Love is the only thing that can make you do something like that."

"How many times do I have to tell you it's over between me and her, you see how I treat her when she comes around harassing us. Call me when you get home to let me know you made it home safely."

When I get home I don't call. I return the car keys to my girl, lay on the couch, cry and pray, "Lord, what have I gotten myself into, I love this man with all of my heart. Lead me and guide me, please let him be the one, please let him love me the way I love him."

I drift off to sleep. Keisha, who heard of the incident that same night from Louis, awakens me with a phone call. "Celeste!"

"Wassup, I was sleeping, Keisha."

"Umm-hmm, well, wake your ass up...I heard about last night.

"That damn Louis can't hold water."

"She is not acting like that for no reason girl, see he knocked her door down."

"Yeah, but he says that they got into an argument and she said something he didn't like. Plus you know how hot tempered he can get." Mitchell is known for being able to get physical when he gets upset. He has never hit a woman, but on his record already he had assaulted a police officer in a club and got into another fight a couple of months before this.

"Why are you making excuses for him? Louis told me it was because another dude was in there."

"He says that is not the case, Keisha."

"Girl, you're crazy! I am just trying to look out for you, something is going on if he is doing stuff like that, you need to be paying attention."

"Okay, Keisha, I'll call you back," I say to end the conversation. Already feeling like shit and not going to class, I get the kids together and drop them off at daycare, which is right around the corner from my house. I always asked God to give me a place where I would always have a babysitter and a daycare that was close, no matter what he always provided.

After dropping off and returning home I call my mom back from leaving her hanging earlier that morning. My mom and I are like best friends at this point; after all we had been through our relationship is unbreakable. "Hey ma," I say in a childish please-don't-ask-what-I-did-last-night voice.

"Hey girl, is everything alright, what happened last night?"

I give her the rundown of everything and she jumps on the boat with Keisha. "Look, Celeste, I will tell you like this, only love will make you do something like that. He is still messing with that girl. I told you she wasn't acting like that for no reason."

All I can do is say, "Okay, ma, I will talk to you later." I hang up the phone and slump back over the couch, thinking, "But I am in love, I haven't told him that but the way he treats me is so good to me and he gives me all of his time, when does he have time to see her.?"

Towards the end of that same summer there is a big concert happening that happens every summer, Summer Fest. The radio station hosts it and all the parties are jumping that night. I am dressed and looking good along with my cousin Meka, 5'7, brown skinned, about my size but her hips are wider than mine, and her friend Donna, about 5'7 also, dark skinned. She lost a lot of weight in the fall so she is about 130; however, she never had a cute face and is the type of friend who will get drunk and do anything. They had come up from my home town to go out with me.

The night is cool and the club is jumping. After the club the police are re-routing traffic and we end up riding past Mitchell and his friends. I can see in his eyes that he is closer to drunk than tipsy so I yell to him to answer his phone. I call him and I say, "I am coming to your house."

"Okay, that's fine," he says.

I have Meka take me to his apartment even though she really doesn't know her way around. She is going to ride on the strip for a minute, then call back for directions. I get out of the car, walk up the steps, and I am thinking it's about to be on and popping. I look good and I know he will think so. I get to the door and I knock but there is no answer. From the outside I hear his roommate Louis knock on his room door and call his name, "Mitchell!" But I cannot hear the rest of the conversation. So I know he is in there.

I stand there knocking and knocking. I call his cell phone, which he is not answering. I call the house phone, which is off the hook, and I call his roommate's cell phone, which he will not answer. So now I am pissed. I have to use the bathroom and I know he is there...why isn't he opening the door?

Finally, a girl comes walking up the steps and she is on a cell phone. I am looking at her and she is looking at me and I am thinking, "What the hell?" When she reaches me at the top of the steps his roommate opens the door and is on the phone with her. I walk in after her and say, "I know you heard me." He does not reply but takes the girl in his room and closes the door.

I approach Mitchell's room, grab the doorknob, and it's locked. BANG BANG BANG! "Open the door...why is the door locked." I yell.

"HOLD ON!!" he yells in a drunken voice.

"I have to use the bathroom. Why is the door locked?" BANG

BANG BANG!!!! I knock again.

"You don't have to bang on the door, I am coming." He opens the door and the light from the TV is shining on a girl with an unfamiliar face sitting on his bed fully clothed. He is in a t-shirt and his boxers.

I remain calm like an Aquarius normally does and I say, "Hello, how are you?" to the girl as I storm through the room to the bathroom. After using the bathroom I wash my hands thinking, "What is about to happen?" as I exit this bathroom. "What are you going to do, Celeste?" I quiz myself. I am not driving, my cell phone is going dead, and Meka doesn't even know her way around. Keisha lives close by...I will walk to her house. Once I get my plan together I dry my hands and walk back into the room.

"I will leave." I started.

"No, I will leave," the girl competes.

"No, you stay. I will leave," I reply.

"You know what? How about we both stay," she suggests.

Now the attention focuses on him as I take a seat on a short burgundy leather stool he has that matches his room. The first thing out of his mouth is, "I didn't try anything with her, Celeste. I didn't try anything with her! Did I try anything with you?" he directs this question to the girl.

"No, but I could have got some if I wanted it. You're drunk," she replies confidently.

"Nah, I don't think so," he replies.

I am sitting, watching their argument, as this brown-skinned, 5'7" 135 pound female is sitting on his bed. She does not have a pretty face but is a whole lot mature than dealing with Trinity.

She introduces herself as Belinda. She is going off on him about how she thought he was different and how he is a liar. He is arguing back at her and just pretty much saying "what-ever".

82

"I am glad you are not crazy," she says as she looks at me.

"Yeah, I am not but he has a crazy one and she is due to pop up any minute now."

Sure enough, three minutes later, BANG BANG BANG at the front door.

"Let me answer it," I say as I jump up.

"No, I will answer it," Belinda competes.

I say okay. I am just staring at him with the first of many stares of disbelief.

In storms Trinity. He is standing in front of his dresser so she sees him first. "Why did you turn your phone off?"

"My phone is not off," he explains.

She looks to the right and sees me sitting on the stool and stares back at him confused. By this time, Belinda walks back in the room and I shout, "Yeah, Trinity, ask her all the questions you ask me. Are they together, does she sleep in his bed, do they go out to eat."

Trinity, not the sharpest knife in the drawer, has no clue as to what is really happening. So she turns and leaves the house after slamming the door.

Now back to the conversation, Belinda starts to claim that Mitchell told her he loved her. Mitchell quickly responds, saying, "I don't love nobody but my mama and my brothers."

Trinity comes storming down the hallway after hearing that. She had slammed the door as if she had left but was sitting on the couch the whole time. "Oh you don't love me!" she yells from one end of the house to the other as she approaches him.

He replies, "I don't love nobody but my mama and my brothers."

"Oh you don't love me, you don't love me!"

Once again he replies, "I don't love nobody but my mama and my brothers."

Storming out of the room once again, Trinity goes into his living room ranting and raving, throwing things around and breaking dishes. At this point I get in touch with Meka to come and get me. Mitchell then runs to the front of the house, Louis now comes out of his room and runs behind him. SMACK!

"I hate you, you don't love me," Trinity slaps the shit out of Mitchell, now they are tussling.

"This is not your house. You won't be breaking anything in here!" Mitchell yells as he grabs her neck pushing her head toward the kitchen sink. Louis grabs Mitchell. Trinity breaks free and runs outside. The girl who came to see Louis locks the door behind her. By this time Belinda and I are trying to pick up what Trinity had thrown down. Mitchell is very angry and frustrated. He quickly gets dressed as everyone else in the house is trying to convince him to calm down and not leave the house.

Trinity comes back, BANG BANG BANG with a crowbar at the door, yelling, "OPEN THE DOOR!!!!"

Mitchell insists on leaving. Louis opens the door and holds Trinity long enough for Mitchell to get to his car. Trinity runs and jumps in her car and they both speed off.

Belinda and I stick around in his apartment parking lot tripping about the whole situation. We exchange numbers and keep in touch a few days after that. The next day she met him at a nearby gas station to get some things she had left at his house that night and they never really talk again after that.

I should follow in her footsteps. At this point I don't know what to think. I am tired of all the drama and what seem to be lies from Mitchell but I have no proof of anything. He explains that Belinda was just some girl he had met about a week before. He claims he didn't even remember telling her to come over, he was drunk.

Knowing how my friends and family feel about the way Trinity is acting and the things I am taking from Mitchell, I decide to keep all incidents to myself. I make a special bottle in my heart to keep them in. I never tell anybody what I am going through with him. Some days I just say to myself "Forget it!" but after a few arguments and some apologizing I am right back in love. I receive nice gifts for every holiday, several outfits from The Limited, and I am impressed.

After graduating from college that year, I am looking for a job. I want to move closer to my mom who is a state away but Mitchell expresses how he is moving back to his home town, which is an hour away. He had graduated a year before me and is also looking for a job. He keeps me posted on job opportunities in his home town and I apply for a couple of them.

Well, I am asked to interview for a teaching position with the county and I jump on it. His mom, Diana Austin a.k.a. Mrs. Di to all the neighborhood kids, is 6 foot tall slim build, very pretty and has the wardrobe of a celebrity, offers me his old bedroom. My kids have not returned from their summer vacation at my son's father's place, so I take her up on the offer.

I am growing up now. I hook up with a relative who give me a hook-up on a way to get a new car from Florida. I ask Mitchell to come home and ride with me to the country to get this car.

"I don't feel like riding all the way down there."

"Mitchell, it's not far and I don't want to go by myself." (I felt like it was far too, but I wanted him to ride with me.)

"Why can't you just get a car from here?"

"Because my credit is not too good and I don't have a down payment. Come on, I am getting a hook-up."

He says okay so we ride to Pensacola, Florida, and get a white Mitsubishi Lancer like the one in The Fast and The Furious movie. I am a big girl now. Mrs. Di helps me get clothes for work and she gives me food or whatever I need. Come to find out all the time I thought Mitchell was spending big money on my gifts he was getting hook-ups from his mom's associates. Slowly things are not what they seem.

CHAPTER 6.

Mystery Man

After living with his mom for about a month I miss my kids and I want them with me. She agrees and they move into his old bedroom with me. Things are still great. Mitchell has not moved home yet. He is still living in the city where we went to school. His lease ends as I am leaving and I keep my apartment to allow a storage space for all of our stuff until I find a place. He is staying between my apartment and his friend's apartment.

Things are great! He comes home on weekends and spends time with me. He is warming up to my kids and talks and plays with them a little more. His mom becomes like my mom. His grandmother keeps my children while I work, for a small fee. His family and I become really close. His mom takes care of us like we are her own. She knows people who could get you whatever you want, from designer bags to designer suits. Soon I learn that everything that Mitchell has in his life he got from a hook-up. I thought they were wealthy people but I thought wrong. His mom could make one phone call and have a new wardrobe if she wanted it.

This teaching position is my first professional position after college and Mrs. Di keeps me fresh. I am feeling great, a computer applications teacher at Ingram Middle School. The majority of the teachers and students are black but, everybody is real cool and down to earth, though. The students are bad as hell but the fact that I am young and keep my appearance up gives them a special respect for me. The worst kids come into my classroom during my planning period and talk me to death about anything. I don't mind, though, at least they feel like they can come to me.

My classroom is my sanctuary. Eight computer tables outline the room holding at least two computers on each, and my workstation is in the middle of this cube. To my right are three large windows making up one of the walls of the room. If the lights are off you can see the reflection on the lightweight steel gates right outside the window that were to keep anyone from getting in and stealing the computers.

Since I am what they call an elective teacher, I teach all grades and the state does not give a lot of weight to my test scores. The state thrives off of the math and reading scores – if they are low your school is considered bad and we are one of those schools. Outside of the school the talk about our school seems bad but I work there...I take pride in it and I love those children.

I have two 8th grade classes in the morning, a 7th grade class right after lunch, and a 6th grade class at the end of the day. I hate 6th graders – they still have the mentality of elementary school kids. I don't hate them individually...I just don't want to deal with them at the end of the day.

In December of that year about 2 months after I got my new car, I receive a phone call from an unusual number. "Hello, may I speak to Celeste?" a stranger asks, as if she is a friend of mine.

"Yes, this is she."

"This is Angela from Pensacola Auto Deals. The deal didn't go through with your car and we need you to bring it back."

Shocked, I stutter, "What?!"

"Yes, the deal didn't go through on your car and we need you to bring it back."

Thinking quickly, I say, "Well you will have to come and get it."

"Okay, ma'am. Well, we can schedule a time."

I hold the phone devastated and a tear drops from my right eye. I try to call Mitchell several times so that he can comfort me but I don't get an answer. Finally, after the third call, he answers, "Wassup."

"Why aren't you answering your phone?"

"I was at the gym playing ball, what's wrong?"

"This lady just called me telling me that I have to turn my car back in," I explain in a crackling crying voice.

"Why?" he asks in a nonchalant tone.

"I don't know. They say the deal didn't go through, what am I gonna do? I don't wanna ask your mom to take me here, take me there, and all of that."

"Oh well, let me call you back," is his reply.

I pause and look at the phone, then press the end button as if to press straight through the phone to his ear. I leave the house and get in the car and ride around for hours. Just riding, crying, and thinking. Feeling alone, this is the first time that I feel that Mitchell doesn't care. He didn't give one word of comfort. I ride and think about this for hours.

Not really knowing my way around the city, I stop at a Food Lion to keep myself from getting too far out and to get some candy I promised to my students. Getting them to answer questions in class is like pulling teeth unless I have something to bribe them with.

I still have on my work clothes, a button-up with different shades of brown in it, plain brown dress pants with a slight crease down the front and back. They fit snug around my hips and waist but are flowing enough to stay professional. I am feeling bad but I stayed looking good, my whole outfit

Mitchell's mom hooked me up with from The Limited.

I walk in the sliding door and walk past the sexiest bald headed man I have ever seen. He is about 6 foot, light chocolate complexion, smooth bald head shining in the grocery store light. His head is shaped just right as to form a perfect face with a tapered mustache and small beard, very neat and clean looking but I can tell he may have just gotten off work. He has on a white tee, some jeans, some socks and Nike flops as if he just ran out of the house to the store quickly. He is talking to the Spanish security guard. I gather bags of Laffy Taffy and Jolly Rancher lollipops and head to the cash register.

I don't think he has noticed me yet so I proceed to walk out of the store. As I walk past the sexy man and the security guard again it is like slow motion, swinging my hair in the air blower from the sliding door, the twist in my walk that makes my butt jiggle just right. I give him a sexy look back as I walk away and if he and the security guard were able to speak the word "DDAAAMMNNN!!!!" would have come flying out of both their mouths. I take my time getting to my car and getting in so that he has time to come out and ask for my number.

As I am getting in the car he starts to exit the store and I notice he has a little boy with him. As I am pulling out of the parking lot as if I'm not waiting for him, he approaches my window. He has the sexiest Jamaican accent I have ever heard. When he speaks I shiver. He asks my name and number and I the same. We exchange and I pull out of the parking lot with him on my mind.

His name is Kevin. He has dark eyes like he can see into my soul. His bald head is just right for rubbing and grabbing, and he has a deep soothing Jamaican tone that turns me on.

I have been gone from the house for about two or three hours now and Mitchell's mom, Mrs. Di, is wondering where I am. I answer her call and inform her about what has happened. Immediately she calls a friend of hers and sets things up for me to go out the next day and get a car.

I am feeling good, just met a new man, and I will be able to get me a new car. Later that night as I am finding my way back to the house Kevin calls. We talk all through the night. He has his own business. He is a contractor, and he could build anything from cabinets to decks. He is in the process of separating from his wife and they are selling the house. They have two children and one on the way. However, one of the children, which was the one who was at the grocery store with him, is not his. He has cared for him from a baby. He explains that he does not love his wife and he married her because she was pregnant.

At the time she is living with a friend and he is still living in the house. He is showing me all the attention that Mitchell is lacking. I am in love with Mitchell and have not expressed it to him. Neither has he expressed it to me. He tells Trinity clearly in front of me and Belinda that night that he only loved his mama and his brothers.

That week Kevin and I see each other every day. We go on a date every night that week. We hit it off. Conversations are stimulating and last forever. I talk to Mitchell less and less that week. I still love him but he is not giving me what I need at the moment.

On Wednesday of that week, Mitchell comes home for a job interview in a small city about 20 minutes away. I ask him to come and visit me at the middle school I work at but he makes excuse after excuse.

"I can't, I wanna get back on the road before traffic hits. I am going to eat lunch with my mama so I won't have time."

Disappointed as usual, I call Kevin as I did every day on my planning period and we make plans for dinner that night. Being that I am staying with Mitchell's mom, I let her know that I am finding a babysitter for that night and I am going

91

on a date at Red Lobster. I guess you can say I do it knowing she will most likely tell Mitchell and at this time I don't care. He is being an asshole, he doesn't have time for me when I need him, what one man won't do another will and vice versa. He can't say that about me because I do everything he wants and more.

Kevin and I meet at Red Lobster, have a nice dinner, then retire to his place. Sitting on the couch thinking the same thing at the same time but using the TV as a focal point, finally he slowly rubs my thigh starting at my kneecap and going north. By the time he gets to the middle of my thigh I want to jump all over him but I play it cool. He leans over to kiss me and it is the most passionate, sexiest kiss I have ever felt. It is the kind that only happens in movies and is enough to say "I do" and he hasn't even popped the question yet.

He pulls me on top of him picks me up like I am as light as a feather. Kissing all the way to the bedroom he lays me down and undresses me slowly. You know when a man is good because he does everything in slow motion. That night I have the best sex ever. Better than any of the sexual experiences with Mitchell. When I think about it I get chills.

The next morning I have to wake up really early to get my kids and make it to work on time. A kiss from his soft brown lips is enough to start a wonderful day. That whole day I am floating. I don't talk to Mitchell that day and I don't even care.

On Friday of that week I am moving out of Mitchell's mom's house and into a new apartment. Of course, Mrs. Di knows somebody who knows somebody who gets me into a nice cheap apartment complex. Mitchell and his brother Randy are moving all of my stuff for me. Randy, who is attending the school of which Mitchell and I are alumni, is 6 foot chocolate tone, I must say sexier than Mitchell, 5 years younger, and has a very strong resemblance to their father. He is also a dog and cheats on his girlfriend numerous times but she can never prove it.

I call Mitchell on my planning period to see what the progress is. He is sounding a little distant and disappointed. "Hey Mitchell, is everything okay?"

"Yes and no."

"Well, what's wrong?"

"Have you wondered why I haven't really been talking to you this week, Celeste?"

"Well, yes." All the time I am thinking I hadn't noticed since I was so busy with Kevin.

He says, "Well, you know on Wednesday when I came for the interview, I used my friend Miguel's car and I followed you. I know that you went on a date with some guy to Red Lobster and I know you ate the seafood combo with the fried shrimp and the scampi with a raspberry lemonade.."

Uh oh, Celeste, busted! "Uh well, you followed me?"

"Yes in Corn's car. Just tell me why you did it!"

"I did it to get your attention, you were ignoring me, you wouldn't come see me at the school, half the time you don't answer your phone when I call."

"If you needed some attention you should have let me know, I love you, Celeste."

Why does he pick now to tell me something like that? There is a pause on the phone while I try to gather my thoughts."

"You do?"

"Yes, I do."

"I love you too, Mitchell, and I am sorry."

So there it is...the first time he tells me he loves me. A year and some change after we met. I am glowing then. But I wish the circumstances were better.

"Well, Mitchell, I needed some attention and I felt like you were tossing me to the side."

He doesn't answer but exhales as if to say that's bullshit.

"So, are you still moving everything?" I ask to switch the subject.

"Yes," he answers with a disappointed voice.

"Okay, well, call me when you get a chance."

Hanging up with Mitchell calling Keisha:

"Girl, Mitchell told me he loves me today. He said he followed me and he knows about Kevin."

"What! He followed you! You have a stalker on your hands. Ha, ha, ha!" she laughs.

"He told me he loved me, girl, did you hear me?"

"Yes, that's good, I guess. So, is he mad about the date?"

"Yeah, he was pretty upset. But I am going to test him. If he delivers all of my stuff and I ask him to stay with me tonight and he does, he must really love me. If he doesn't, then it's not meant to be.

"Okay, well call me and let me know the verdict."

"You know I will, girl"

That night Mitchell and his brother moved all of his stuff and mine out of my old apartment in Tuskegee, Alabama and into my new three bedroom apartment about five minutes away from his mom's house in Phoenix City, Alabama. At this time, I am only using two of my bedrooms because my daughter doesn't have her own bed yet, so I let him put all of his stuff in my third bedroom. This includes a bed, two couches, the living room table set, and a truckload of clothes and shoes. When the truck is almost unloaded and I catch him outside alone I am about to ask him to stay when he opens his mouth first and volunteers, "Do you want me to stay with you tonight so that I can help you straighten up?"

"Yes, I was just about to ask you if you would."

"Sure I will."

I smile as I walk away carrying another item in the house thinking, "This is meant to be."

As weeks pass, things get better. He answers when I call.

He comes home just about every weekend.

I see Kevin one other time after that. He asks me to go out to eat with him to this Chinese place that we used to go to. By this time a few months have passed and now Mitchell is back on track, but I can't resist. Kevin asks me to come and pick him up so that we can ride together, but I hear the kids in the background so I ask, "Is your wife there?"

"Yeah, but she knows it's over, it's cool, come and get me."

Hesitant, I reply, "I don't think that will be a good idea, maybe we should just go another time."

"No, no, it's nothing like that, she knows that," he insists.

"Okay, I am on my way."

Pulling up in front of the house I call him to come out. She comes out first, acting as if she is getting something out of the car. She is about 5'6, really dark-skinned, small frame, wearing a ragged tee shirt and some dirty looking jeans. She must have been coming to pick up some stuff. She looks over at me and I am looking at her like, "What!"

He comes out a few seconds later. She is fussing at him as he approaches my 2003 frog green Saturn Ion, which I am proud to have thanks to Mrs. Di. He gets in and we pull off as if she was never there. We pull into the shopping center with a Bi-Lo grocery store to my left alongside a nail shop and Hallmark store. Across the parking lot was the restaurant, Great China. We pull up to park in front of the building when she pulls up beside us in some champagne colored four-door sedan.

"Hold on a sec," he says as he gets out of the car.

"So that's how you gonna do it!" she shouts, "just disrespect me like that."

I am in the car thinking, "Oh hell, here we go."

I place my car into reverse about to leave his ass right there. When I put my car into gear the doors automatically lock. The locking sound of the doors makes him look back and motion for me to get out of the car. She pulls out of the parking space, and the tires screech as she pulls off.

Sitting down at the table the atmosphere is very awkward. I have to break the silence by saying, "I told you I didn't want to come and get you like that."

"Well, she needs to know it's over, you acting all scared!"

"Scared! Don't use me to let her know...you need to do that on your own time."

"Hi, I am Samere, your server. What can I get for you tonight?"

"Let's just get this to go," he says in a stern voice.

Cutting my eye at him and trying to maintain my composure in the restaurant I order my usual, Sesame Shrimp. It had become my favorite Chinese dish and I had only heard of it by going there with him, but now that didn't matter because this is the last time I would be going anywhere with him. We ride in silence back to his house and he gets out of the car without saying a word.

I am holding my lips together because I know I am going to cuss him out if they are to pop open. After that we talk a few more times but that is the last time I see him. I am maintaining my love for Mitchell and so far no drama from Trinity. Everything is going great until he is getting prepared to move back home. I ask him to move in with me as it would help me out on bills but he insists on living with his 19 year old brother who is transferring schools back to a school in their home town to follow his girlfriend who he is still cheating on. Their relationship is confusing; Mitchell and I just laugh about it.

Mitchell and I are having constant arguments about a title. "What's the difference if we have a title or not, it won't change anything, Celeste!"

"Yes it will," I argue.

"What will it change? We will still do the same things we do

96

now," he debates.

"If a title makes no difference then why have you ever had a girlfriend in your life. Why did you have a title with them but won't have one with me.?"

"It's not that I don't want one but I don't think it's necessary right now."

This becomes an ongoing shouting match between us on a 2- to 3-day basis. It is weird to me because we have never disagreed about anything before. The arguments sometime end up with me crying and very emotional and they almost always end up in that good make-up sex.

"Is a title all you need, girl!" he would shout as he smacked me on my ass.

"Hell no, I need this dick!" I would yell back as I would throw my voluptuous booty back to his waistline making a loud clapping noise. I loved it when he would hit it from the back.

Now moving in slow motion, sweaty and relieved from the energy that has been released from our souls, he bends down to kiss my lower back as if to say, "This is my pussy." Positioning ourselves alongside each other in a manner that he holds me tight from behind, he whispers, "I love you,"

"I love you too, baby."

He kisses my cheek and we go to sleep. It doesn't matter what happened the moment before this, all that matters is us.

CHAPTER 7.

Mitchell Moves Home

Mitchell was always confused on what he wanted his career path to be. He did the graphics thing, then he was a bouncer at a club for a few months and found himself wanting to open up one, then he was thinking of owning his own security team. Now his newest venture is deciding he wants to be a loan real estate agent. He doesn't want to take a class like normal people do – he decides he can teach himself with the proper books. He goes over his friend's house and swears he is studying and he can't answer the phone because his signal is always out.

Some days we go to the park and I help him study using note cards he created. I am drilling him almost every day and he seems to have the information sketched in his head pretty well. The test is $100.

He feels he is ready after two months of studying so he signs up to take the test. I drill him with questions until the very hour before the test. I am sure that he has it. WRONG!

The kids and I go to Mrs. Di's a couple of nights a week to eat dinner, because she cooks every day. Pulling up in front of her house, I see Mitchell's truck is there. I am excited thinking, "Yes! He must have passed the test...he seems to be back early."

I open the screen door to knock on a heavy brown wooden door, stained glass in a square shape forming four window panes. His younger brother opens the door. He is 11 years old, a skin tone that is in between light and dark; he is sort of golden. He is about my height but getting taller by the minute. Close haircut and light brown eyes, slender but not skinny, he is a good kid, but has the potential to act up. He is not disrespectful but sneaky, he needs to fit in with neighborhood kids and schoolmates. "Wassup punk!" which is a normal greeting between me and him. He is like my little brother and I would do anything for him.

I walk through a small living room with the type of furniture that you did not sit on. This leads to a bright light that is the kitchen. Mrs. Di recently had the kitchen remodeled after Mitchell and Randy moved out, it was something she always wanted to do. She threw out an old kitchen table and placed an electric stove in the middle of the floor – the kind that has the flat top for the eyes and space on the other side for dining with bar stools around it, gray and cream marble designer kitchen floors that match the cream counter tops and cabinets with gray handles. The refrigerator is one of the big steal two-door refrigerators with an icemaker. Just to the right of the kitchen is a black wine rack filled with wine from different countries. However, the kitchen is not that big – it is a regular sized kitchen but she did her thing with it.

The kids run to the back to play with Mitchell's little brother and I walk into the kitchen. He is sitting on the gray color seat barstool with his head in his hands. "Hey baby!" I shout with a happy please-tell-me-you-passed-the-test voice.

"I didn't pass the test, babe," he says in a very disappointed voice.

Standing on my tip-toes and throwing my right arm around him, I kiss him on his cheek, "You will pass it next time, baby, don't worry. Just study a little bit harder, it will come to you."

The test is $150 every time he takes it. He fails it four times, I even pay for the test once. His family and friends have given up on him. They tell him he is crazy but I try my best to keep him encouraged.

On the fifth try, I decide to plan a surprise for him. Whether he passes it or not I am going to give him something he can feel. I tell him to come and get me that night after the test so that I can ride with him to his mom's to eat dinner. I send the kids to church with his grandmother. I go to the Dollar Store and buy twelve candles. I put three on the kitchen table to the right of my front door, two on the bar to the left, two on the dresser to the left of the entrance to my room, three on the night table to the left of my bed which was directly in front of the dresser, and two on the bathroom counter. Since the bathroom is inside my room the candles are shining from the bathroom into my room.

That night he comes over right after the test is over. I leave the door unlocked for him to enter. When he comes in I have the candles lit, old-school music is playing, and I am laid across the bed with a sexy black see-through lacy cami, the underwear to match, and black heels. When he comes in the door he is speechless. I approach him and the passion starts. That night, what has been sex turns into making love. He loves me slow and kisses me softly and whispers, "I love you" as we reach the point of orgasm at the same exact time. It is mind-blowing for both of us.

From that day on, sexually we are on a different level. Oh yeah, he passed the test. Now he has a plan and is ready to move back home. I ask him to move in with me but he prefers to live with his mom until him and Randy can find a place, plus he has no job and no money. He doesn't want to seem as if he is living off of me. I don't mind – I volunteer to take care of him, but I can respect his point of view.

However, I find myself giving him $50 to $100 a week just because I love him and I know he doesn't have any money. After finding that the real estate thing wasn't working he wants to start a non-profit organization for retired veterans: $400 for the book and the class on how to start and run a professional non-profit agency. He has no means of taking this class. He is going to borrow the money from his grandmother who has been retired for years and is barely paying for her own expenses. I don't want that to happen plus I am in a position to help so I volunteer with no problem. He promises to pay me back but realistically, how is he going to do that? $400 I pay for him to take that class and he fails the class exam by, like, 20 points. This means he fails the class and will have to pay $100 to take the exam again. Soon he gives up on this dream also.

I pay for everything we do on every date and I don't mind because I love him. In a conversation about how much we love each other, he lets me know that he is grateful for everything I am doing for him. He confesses that he loves me more than anyone he had ever been with. He says, "I don't know what I would do if I saw you with somebody else."

Quick on my feet, I reply, "But I thought you had already seen me with somebody else!"

"I, I mean I did, I am just saying I don't know what I would do if I saw you with anybody else again."

Once again, things are not what they seem. After pondering for a while about the incident where he said he followed me, I figure out that his mom told him where I went and he could describe what I ate at the restaurant because I always order the same thing. If he followed me, why didn't he see us go back to Kevin's place that night? I never mentioned it to him or Mrs. Di but I was slowly seeing that she could take care of me as much as possible but she is always going to take her son's side. She knows about the drama with Trinity and she would say things like, "Girl, I know he is my son but I wouldn't put up with that." I guess I can't blame her for looking out for her son. I guess her being loyal to her son was more important regardless of how close she and I were.

A couple of months after he moves home he informs me that Trinity has decided to move back home too. They are from the same city but didn't meet until college. She graduates the winter after she was supposed to, with course work in fashion design she has to be a dummy...how hard could that be? Sure enough the next week after he moves home, she moves home, and the drama starts again.

I am at his mom's for dinner one night. His grandmother, Anna Austin, Grandma Ann is what we called her, 5"8, pretty brown wrinkled skin, short hair in the form of a girl and turned completely gray without a trace of black. I think it is so beautiful. She has the heart of a lion. She does not drive because she was in a terrible accident when she was a teenager. Mitchell often gets mad when she asks him to take her places at the last minute. But she is his heart; sometimes I believe he loves her more than his mom. She loves my children and me like we are her grandchildren. Faithful to the church and God, and one of the sweetest women I know, she always gets home late from church. She will have one of the members at the church come and get her and drop her off.

This particular night she comes in the house a little shaken up. She speaks of seeing a red car parked behind my car, which pulled off once she pulled up. Trinity drives a 95 red-burgundy Volkswagen Jetta. I know who it is and so does Mitchell even though he tries to play like he doesn't hear what they are saying. His mother goes to look out of the door and she sees paper on the windshield of my car and Mitchell's car. She goes and gets the papers and reads them once she gets back into the house.

The note on Mitchell's car reads, "I see now, Mitchell, you

102

don't have to lie to me about why you're not answering your phone." The note on my car reads, "Congratulations, Celeste, you finally got him." His mom and I laugh but Mitchell never moves from his spot in his room on the bed watching TV.

As I sit down on the bed beside Mitchell, all of a sudden my cell phone rings. It's Trinity, asking, "Why do you keep messing with my man?" I look at the phone and hang it up. She calls right back. "Look, bitch, don't be hanging up on me!"

I cut her off and immediately ask, "Where are you? Are you outside? I am tired of your bullshit and I am ready to whip your ass. Are you outside?"

"Yes, I am!"

"Well, I am on my way."

As I hop up off the bed to get to the door Mitchell runs to the door first. "Chill out! What's wrong with you? You don't need to be fighting – you are a teacher."

By this time, Trinity is banging on his mother's door. His grandmother is asking me to calm down and pray. I want to say, "Grandma, I don't wanna pray right now...I wanna beat her ass." But I can't disrespect her like that.

Mrs. Di pushes him out of the way of the front door and opens the door cussing at Trinity. "You are not bringing this shit in my house, Trinity, take your ass back outside." Because of the past between Mitchell and Trinity, Mrs. Di doesn't like her and does not allow her to come to the house. She mentioned to me that during their relationship Trinity tried to kill herself because Mitchell wanted to break it off, Trinity's mom blamed Mitchell, and Mrs. Di had had a bad taste in her mouth for Trinity ever since.

Mitchell pushes past his mom and pushes Trinity out of the door and closes the door behind him. Grandma is still trying to pray with me and holding on to my wrist, but I am really not feeling it right now. But I respect her too much to jerk away, run out the back door to the front, and whip Trinity's ass.

103

"I wanna go home, let me go home," I repeat as I walk toward the door.

Mitchell comes back in the house as I approach the door. "Wait a minute, just wait a minute before you leave."

"This is all your fault. You let her do this shit and I can't take it anymore!" I yell at him frustrated and confused.

Mitchell covers the door so that I cannot get out. "Why do you want to fight? Chill out! You got too much to lose."

At this point what I have to lose is not on my mind. Grandma Ann starts to whimper and pray. "See the pain you cause?" I say as I roll my eyes at Mitchell. His stance softens as he glances over at his grandmother. She wants us to work more than we do. She is always advocating for us to get married. I look at him with a stare of disgust and push past him out of the door and to my car.

Trinity has pulled off by then but she calls my cell phone again.

I answer: "Look bitch, pull your ass over, I have been really nice to you and it's because of Mitchell but I am tired of your shit!" I scream. "Where are you?! Where are you?!" I scream repeatedly.

"Whatever, you fat bitch!" she replies.

"I will be a fat bitch BUT I am a fat bitch with Mitchell and a fat bitch fucking Mitchell! Kiss my ass!" Slamming the phone down furiously I wish I could find her and really beat her ass right now. Going home I pace around my couch for about five minutes before I calm down. I grab one of my many diaries and begin writing:

I need to write.
Laying awake my mind's too busy I can't sleep at night,
I need to write.
My kids have two different fathers,
one who is willing to take care of both

and one who is always making excuses
and stays broke,
I need to write.
My heart has been broken
because the one I love won't admit
that he doesn't want to commit,
I need to write.
It's getting harder every day in
drama dealing with his ex-girlfriend,
if I see her again we are gonna have to fight,
I need to write.
Thoughts running through my head,
my feelings dripping from my eyes,
feeling like I don't want to try,
I need to write.
So many things bottled inside,
thinking this bottle is about to get too full to hide,
explode it just might,
I need to write.
Walking around with my smile as my vail,
calming my anger and frustration with every exhale,
doing my job and being polite,
that's why I have to, I must,
I need to write.

It is the only thing that can get me calm enough to sleep, then I get into bed second guessing myself. "What is really going on here, Celeste? Am I being just as stupid as she is?" I drift off to sleep with a hundred thoughts running through my mind.

About an hour later Mitchell crawls into bed beside me, holding me, repeating "I am sorry baby."

"I am tired of this shit, Mitchell," I whisper as a tear falls down my cheek.

"I know, baby, I know," wiping my tears away. We both drift off to sleep.

The next day my mind is racing again so I ask, "How did she get my number? The only way she could have gotten the number was out of your phone so when were you with her?"

"I have not been with her," he argues as he jumps out of bed and gets dressed. It's a Friday morning so I had to get dressed for work.

"When were you so comfortable around her that you layed your phone down?"

He answers, "I don't know, I haven't been around her." Everything coming out of his mouth sounds like blah blah blah.

"When is the last time you have seen her?!"

"Well, well, me and my brother helped her move into her apartment."

"WHAT!!" I shout as I threw a pillow at his head. "When, and why didn't you tell me about it?"

"We were mad at each other at the time and we weren't talking that day."

"SO how many other things have you done on days we get mad at each other, Mitchell?"

"All I did was help her move...nothing else."

"So did you lay your phone down then?"

"I don't know, I might have."

"Long enough for her to go through it?"

"That's the only time I have seen her."

We go back and forth for thirty minutes about what the hell he is doing helping her move. I let it go because I have to get to work, but I am mad at him the whole day. I will not answer his phone calls so he comes up to my job with a bouquet of pink roses. He knows that pink is my favorite color...he knows what to do to soften me up.

CHAPTER 8.

The Truth Comes Out

Life goes on, months go by with no sign of drama from Trinity, things are cool. He has gotten a job at the Nike Factory on the production line so he has enough money to move out of his mom's house. He decides that he would rather move in with Randy than move in with me. I tell him that he is making a mistake and it is not wise for him to move in with his brother. He refuses to move in with me saying that he wants to really get on his feet first. Okay cool, whatever. We see each other every day, he seems pretty cool with the kids even though it's going on two years and he has never been to one of their birthday parties. I look around that and I am feeling like he loves me even though some of his stories don't add up. If he doesn't answer the phone he swears he fell asleep. He promises to come see me but won't come until 1 or 2 in the morning. But we stay talking on the phone during the day; whenever I get a free moment I call him and vice versa.

The summer comes and teachers don't get paid in the summer so I decide that I will go to bartending school. Mitchell is totally against it. He expresses this by saying, "I don't want my girl working in a bar with all these men trying to holla at her. I don't agree with it and I don't want anything to do with it, don't even talk to me about it."

"I am trying to make extra money. How dare you come at me like that when you failed that loan officer test several times and everybody was telling you to give it up? I stood behind you and encouraged you even though I didn't agree. So you should give me the same respect! Look, I will talk to you later," I say in a frustrated voice as I hang up the phone.

We don't talk the whole day until dinner time at Mrs. Di's. He opens the door to let the kids and me in and starts by saying, "I, I apologize, you're right. I don't agree but I will support you." Hugging and kissing we leave that argument at the front door and carry on as usual.

So I get my bartending license and am blessed to have a club owner give me a chance right away. I start off working on the black night in a white night club, which gives me a lot of experience. I am making at least $100 in that one night so I can't complain. It's extra money. Then I take a chance and walk into a strip club, talk to the bar manager, give her my resume, and start working the next weekend. I have to get a sitter to keep my children. Who but Grandma Ann – it is perfect. It starts off as working just weekends, then I pick up some extra days to keep a good cash flow. I am working Wednesday through Saturday bringing home at least $100 each night. I get familiar with the regular customers and some of the girls and my tips grow. I am paying his grandmother $40 a night. I ask Mitchell to watch the kids for me so that I won't have to pay but he refuses. On nights she is busy I have to ask her to ask him to do it just so he will say yes. I go to work at 9; my kids are in the bed by then and all I need him to do is sit there with them. He still refuses.

Mitchell and I get into an argument about the kids. "Why haven't you ever been to one of my kid's birthday parties?!" I shout.

"They don't know whether I am there or not!" he shouts

back.

"Yes, they do, kids are not stupid. Maybe they think you don't care about being there."

"Those kids are not thinking about me and whether or not I am there. They don't look at me as their daddy, I don't have any kids."

"They don't look at you that way because you don't act anything close to a daddy, and you do have kids. If you're gonna be with me you have step kids and if you can't deal with that, then you can't be with me, know what."

"Baby, calm down, calm down," he says in that tired same old sweet soft voice. "You know I want you and everything that comes along with it. I love you."

"I love you, too," I say as his words turn me into mush.

"It's okay, we can work anything out," he explains.

I think so too. At this point I believe that we can. Things are so wonderful – I am in love like never before. I will do anything he asks me. Months are passing by with no drama from Trinity, and I am searching for clarification on the relationship that is growing between me and Mitchell. He will make comments that I am his girl, and we talk about marriage and even having a baby in the near future.

"Title? We don't need no title, what's the difference?" he argues.

"A title is important. If it isn't, why does anybody ever have a title on a relationship?" I cry.

"What does it change, Celeste? A title means nothing," he repeats.

Sitting on the other end of a phone line, I cry silently.

"We don't need a title," he shouts, "and don't ask me about it again! When it is time we both have to be ready."

Getting off the phone I call my mom for comfort. "Celeste, my advice is the same as it has been since all the drama started with that other girl. You need to leave him alone. He is still messing with that girl."

"Ma, no, he is not. I haven't had any drama in a while. I am stuck on this title thing. He feels that we don't need one but it's important to me. You won't listen to me and I have nothing else to say about it. BYE MA!"

"Bye," she answers calmly.

Mitchell then calls back, "Baby, I am sorry for the shouting, I hate fighting with you, you know we are together. What does a title have to do with it?"

"So we are together?"

"We have always been together. A title doesn't make or break us."

Drying up my tears I say, "Okay, baby." A feeling of comforting love comes over my whole body. Like a heated blanket when it's 30 degrees outside, I am so comfortable in knowing that he is mine. I am more than in love with this man than I have ever been with anyone. He completes me, he is my everything.

Months are still passing by and things are perfect, no sign of Trinity. Mitchell and I see each other every day, eating lunch with each other every day that we can. Sometimes I leave school on my planning period and meet him down the street at Jack Sprat's Café. He always orders the meatball sub and I the crabmeat salad. He always knows what I want and I always know just what he needs, it is great.

"For Sisters Only" weekend is coming up. This means big parties and lots of people. I am still bartending every week so I am unable to attend the after party at the Hyatt Hotel. However, Mitchell is able to be on the scene along with his friend, Tommy, who came from out of town, and his friends, Corn and Jacob.

When I get home from work that Saturday night about 2:30 a.m., I call Mitchell. I figure the club is out by now but he doesn't answer his phone. I take a shower and get in bed as usual. For some strange reason I wake up exactly 30 minutes later and the first thing on my mind is to call Mitchell. Grabbing my phone, drained from work, I listen to it ring and wait for him to answer. "Come pick me up from the Hyatt!" he answers in an excited tone.

Not asking any questions I say, "Okay," and hang up the phone and immediately start to get dressed. Not knowing what is going on I am rushing to get to him when I receive a phone call from Jacob asking excitedly, "Are you coming to get him man?"

"I am on my way, Jacob, I am on my way!"

Jumping in my car, speeding down the freeway to get to him, Corn calls me, "Are you coming to get him man! Come and get this fool man!"

"I am coming, Corn, I am coming!" Now I am nervous, what the hell is going on, the butterflies in my stomach are about to bust out and fly out the window if I don't make sure my man is okay, doing 75 in a 55 miles per hour zone.

As soon as I reach the exit to get to the Hyatt, a call from Mitchell comes through. "That's okay, don't come and get me," he says in an aggravated voice.

"I am right here, I am getting off on the exit."

"I am with John, don't worry. Say something, John." John can barely say a word before Mitchell snatches the phone back away from his mouth. "See, I am with John." John is one of the guys that Mitchell used to play basketball with him in the gym at school, he had come down to party.

"Okay, okay, well, what happened? What's wrong? What's going on?"

"John has a room here at the hotel. I am here, I am going to stay here with him."

"Okay." Hanging up the phone, puzzled, I continue on to the hotel. RING! RING! My cell phone again.

"Come pick me up, man, come pick me up!"

111

"Okay, baby, I am almost there, I am almost there! Stay there!"

As I approach the hotel entrance I see a car pulling out of the hotel. In the car two girls are in the front and two guys are in the back. One of the guys looks just like Mitchell, so I u-turn and start to follow them. Calling and calling Mitchell's phone...he does not answer. I start blinking my lights and blowing my horn at the car to get it to stop as I am repeatedly calling Mitchell and getting no answer.

"Hello," he answers in a drunk, sick voice.

"Where are you!?"

"I am in the hotel."

"This looks like you in this car."

"I am in the hotel."

So I u-turn to go back to the hotel. "Well, I am in front of the hotel, come out." I sit in front of this hotel for 30 minutes at four in the morning and Mitchell never comes out. I call his cell phone over and over but I get no answer. I run into the hotel to search for him, but he is nowhere to be found. Knowing that he is drunk, I assume he caught a ride back to his apartment. As I arrive at his apartment Corn calls yelling, "I am never going out with these fools again!"

"What happened?"

"Mitchell and Tommy started fighting in the club, Tommy turned over the table and walked out. Mitchell walked out after him and these fools were wrestling in the parking lot. Mitchell punched out somebody's headlight in their car and I was going crazy ready to go. Oh, my gosh!!"

I laugh. "Tommy and Mitchell always fight like that after getting drunk," I explain to Corn.

"Yeah, but I don't like that shit."

"Okay, where is Mitchell? I am sitting at his house waiting on him."

"Let me find out and I will call you back."

Now sitting in front of Mitchell's place I notice that his brother is home. I knock on the door for about 5 minutes but it is 5 in the morning so I can only expect so much. Randy and his girlfriend are in the house sleeping with their cell phones off. Corn calls and says, "Mitchell is riding around with John and some girl. I don't know what's going on, but if you want to chill with the rest of us, we are at the Waffle House."

"Nah, I am going home but thanks." I retire to my house around 5:30 a.m. uneasy and feeling confused.

The next morning I wake up, still confused and tired. I call Mrs. Di asking if she has heard from Mitchell. "No, the job is calling here looking for him because he agreed to work some overtime," she explains. "I will ride over to his house to see if he is there." When she gets to the house Randy opens the door and Mitchell is not home. Randy plays a message for her from Corn explaining that Mitchell was drunk and acting stupid at the club, and asking could Randy come get him. As the message comes to an end Mitchell is walking through the door with blood on his shirt from busting his hand by punching the light out of somebody's car.

Mrs. Di starts to get upset, crying, "I don't want my sons to end up being drunks." Their family has a history of drunks. "That's not how I raised my sons to be."

Mitchell, brushing it off and angry at Randy for letting her hear the message, hurries to get dressed and get on his way to work. On his way to work he calls me.

"Hello!"

"Hey baby," he says calmly.

"Where are you?"

"On my way to work now."

"What happened last night? Why didn't you answer me Why didn't you call me back?"

"I just didn't want you questioning about everything that happened."

113

"What! I called you several times and I sat at your at house waiting for you to arrive."

"I told you I was with John, everything is cool. Me and Tommy just got into it at the club. You know how we do, it was nothing major. Corn was tripping."

"Oh, okay," I reply letting it go in a sigh.

"Well, I am pulling up at work, I will call you back."

Hanging up the phone, I am still feeling a little uneasy but I believe him, he loves me, why would he lie? The week starts and we are operating as usual.

The next weekend I am up washing clothes and doing my Saturday duties when Keisha calls me. "Girl wassup, what are you doing?" she starts before I can even say hello good.

"Nothing, just a couple of chores, wassup?"

"Why didn't you tell me what happened last weekend at the club between Mitchell and Tommy."

"What did you hear happened?" I asked, wondering if the story would change. She told the story just as I had heard it from Corn but added one major detail. "Yeah, and I heard Trinity picked him up."

"WHAT!!!"

"Yes, and I heard that he is with her now and not messing with you anymore. She doesn't want him and has tried to talk to other guys but every time she does, Mitchell does something crazy."

"WHAT!!!" is the only thing that can come out of my mouth. I am in a state of shock. ""I will call you back, I will call you back."

"No, no, see, I didn't want to tell you, just keep in mind that you didn't hear it from me."

"Okay," I shout as I almost hang up on her before she can finish her sentence.

I immediately call Mitchell. "Hey baby," he answers.

Without hesitation I ask, "Did Trinity pick you up from the

Hyatt?"

"Huh? What, what are you talking about?" he stutters.

I can tell I caught him off guard. "Did Trinity pick you up from the Hyatt last weekend, Mitchell?" I ask again in slow stern tone.

"Who told you that? Who told you that?"

"It doesn't matter who told me...answer the question."

He gets angry and keeps asking who told me. "If you can't tell me who told you, why would you even call and ask?"

I am not entertaining any of his comments, I am sticking to the question at hand, "Did Trinity pick you up from the Hyatt?"

"No, she did not pick me up but I saw her that night, I told you I was with John, he had a room at the Hyatt and I stayed with him."

We argue back and forth that entire day over who told me. I didn't care to reveal so he starts to put his foot in his mouth. It was probably Kelly, she probably heard something at that beauty salon. Trinity's best friend Tierra does my friend Kelly's hair and is always talking junk behind Trinity's back in the beauty salon. Talking about how much she hates going out with Trinity because she is always running behind Mitchell.

After he makes this comment I get quiet. "Hello!" he shouts.

"Yes, I am here," I answer. "If nothing happened, why would Tierra have anything to tell Kelly?" I ask in a very inquisitive tone.

"Whatever, you won't tell me who told you, I will talk to later."

I say okay and the phone call ends. All that night, this conversation stays on my mind. That Monday Mitchell and I go to eat lunch with his mom and her husband, as we do every Monday. At the table I am feeling like a stranger. I don't have much of an appetite and I feel like everyone at the table

115

knows something I don't. I am very quiet, which is unusual for me.

That night I decide to investigate. Being that I have a computer science degree, I can find out anything I want to know about anybody on the computer. All I need is the Internet and some time to search. The Lord works in mysterious ways because it doesn't even take me 30 minutes to find Trinity's home number.

Nervous to call, I have my son's little cousin call and ask for Trinity and leave her name as Amber. The girl answers the phone. "Can I speak to Trinity?"

The girl consults with Trinity and Trinity yells,

"Who is it, who is this?" the girl asks.

"This is Amber."

"It's Amber."

"Tell her I will call her back!" Trinity shouts.

"She says she will call you back."

Amber and I are in shock on the other end like what's really going on, but later I find that Trinity has a sister named Amber on her dad's side. At this point I don't want to play games...I want to know what's going on. I wait about 15 minutes and I call back myself. This time Trinity answers.

"Hello, Trinity, this is Celeste, do you know who I am."

Considering we have had numerous arguments, she recognizes my voice. "What do you want?" she asks in an aggravated voice.

"I just have one question, did you pick Mitchell up from the Hyatt last Saturday night?"

"Why? Why are you always trying to mess with my man?"

"Excuse me?" I reply, puzzled. "Mitchell and I are together."

She gasps as if her mouth had fallen to the ground.

"Did you pick him up from the Hyatt?"

Now humbling herself she answers, "Yes, I did and he stayed with me."

116

"He told me that he was with John."

A moment of silence passes on both ends of the phone and the next thing you know, Trinity and I discuss the last three years of arguments we had with each other like women. Trinity spoke of nights he was with her and not with me. I revealed lies he told to her. In our conversation we find that Mitchell lives a double life. He knows us very well. He takes us to the same restaurants, buys us the same gifts on holidays and birthdays. He buys us the exact same stuffed animals and gives us the exact same greeting cards. He also goes as far as to sign them the same, "with love, Mitchell." It is funny and painful all at the same time.

"Let me call him on three way," I volunteer just to prove my point.

"Hey baby," he answers calmly.

"Mitchell," I shout, "are you messing with Trinity?!"

"NO!! Why do you ask, I don't wanna talk about her."

"Do you love her?"

"NO!!! I have told you that before."

"Do you love me?"

"Why are you asking me all these questions, wassup?"

"Nothing, just tell me do you love me."

"Of course I do, baby, wassup, why are you asking me all of this?"

"I will call you right back," I say abruptly. Hanging up with him, I yell, "Trinity, are you there?"

"Yes."

"Did you hear that?"

"Yes, hold on," she replies. She calls him on three way on her end just to prove her point.

"Hello," he answers.

"Mitchell," she calls, "are you messing with Celeste?"

"Why are you asking me this? I don't want to talk about her."

117

"Are you messing with Celeste?"

"No, I told you that."

"Tell me you love me.

"You know I love you, Trinity."

"I will call you back." Hanging up on him, we both sit in a state of shock.

I call him back screaming, "I hate you, I heard everything you just said, telling her you love her and you're not with me. I hate you, I don't want to talk to you anymore!"

Returning to the line with Trinity, I advise her, "He has a key to my house. I know he is on his way, so why don't you come over here and meet him. Then we can all talk." Giving her the directions to my house and my address the plan is set. Being that I only live about 5 minutes away from him I only have about ten minutes to throw as much of his stuff off the back balcony of my apartment as I can before he gets here. I am feeling so many emotions at one time that I don't know what is going on. I am hurt, mad, sad, and at the same time happy to finally know the truth.

Tears are pouring down my face. I want to yell but nothing will come out so I go to the room where all his stuff is and I start with his shoes. Tossing as many boxes of them as I can, then his dishes, the plates are cracking and the glass is breaking in the wet grass behind my house. As I go for some papers he busts in the front door. At the same time the phone rings and it's Mrs. Di. "I hate your son!" I scream in a frustrated and a crying trembling voice. "I hate him!"

"What's wrong, what's wrong?!" she yells.

"He was messing with Trinity all this time and..."

Before I can finish my sentence he is in front of me grabbing the phone and hanging up with his mom. My kids are waking up and getting out of bed. "Go back to bed!!!!" he shouts to them. They get back into bed while he tries to explain. Now I'm in the closet trying to grab more of his stuff. He grabs me, hugging me, repeating, "I love you, I love you."

"NO!! Leave, get out! Why! Why! Why did you do this to me!!!" I cry. "Why!!! I was there for you!!! Anything you wanted!!! Why!!!"

"Please," he whispers, "calm down, I love you, I love you."

He tries to kiss me and hug me and explain how much he loves me. "We were talking about having a baby, Celeste, please don't do this." After twenty minutes of me crying and him explaining, things calm down and he notices all of the stuff I have thrown over the balcony. "Celeste, you didn't have to do that."

"Yes, I did."

"Please help me get it from outside it rained today."

"Nope, Trinity will be here any minute and we are going to talk about this."

"What!" his face drops and he hurries outside to gather his things from the grass below the balcony. I am thinking to myself, "Where is Trinity, she should have been here by now, she only lives about 10 minutes away." He gathers the things I had thrown and hurries to his car to flee the scene before Trinity gets here.

I call Trinity. She says she went to the wrong house. I give her directions again and she finally comes about five minutes after he left. She walked in to the house and was in a state of shock when she got to the back room and saw all of his things in my house. Things he told her were at his mom's friend's house. We begin to talk again. I tell her how he came over begging and pleading with me. How he mentioned us having a baby.

"What!! You were talking about having a baby?" she asks in amazement.

"Yes, that's how serious it was," I explained.

"He knows I don't want any children," she replied. "Not right now, anyway." She turns her head and glances into my room.

"He gave me that same teddy bear," she says with disgust.

I wanted to break down crying but I can't do it in front of her. Even though I am sure she is probably hurt, too, she is still my enemy. As we are in the living room talking my son comes out of the kids' room.

"That's your son?"

"Yeah."

"Oh he's cute."

She stays for about five to ten more minutes, then she leaves. I wait about twenty minutes and I call her. "Have you talked to him?"

"Yes, he is standing right here."

"Is he telling you the same things he was telling me?"

Trinity is unable to respond when Mitchell grabs the phone from her and says, "You know what I told her. I told her that I love her way more than I love you."

In a state of shock and total disappointment but wanting to act as if I don't care, I shout, "Well why didn't you tell me that?"

"I am telling you now."

Hanging up the phone, suddenly I feel like I can't breath, like someone has taken a knife that is already stuck in my heart and thrusted it deeper. I fall to the floor gasping for air, crying, "Oh God!!! Oh God help me, please God help me...Why Lord!!! Why!!!!!" I want to die...I have never felt so bad in my life...I continuously pray for comfort, I can hardly see through my teary eyes when I notice my pen and pad on the floor beside me. I grab it and started to write:

Standing still life in slow motion a pain
coming from my left breast,
my shirt soaked in blood,
head sweating tears flowing,
I am dying for sure.

How could this be,
it's too early for me, to die,
to feel this, now feeling sick on the stomach,
the blood was running down
my chest dropping of the floor
forming a perfect puddle.
Thoughts racing, chasing excuses for
the reasons why I am dying.
The trickle from my heart is slowing down.
It is understood in my mind that
when the heart is empty the end is here.
I fall beside this puddle of blood
which is now mixed with tears
and I find that I am no longer in the
house but outside on a cold concrete.
With the small amount of sound
I had left in my soul
I scream WHERE ARE YOU LORD!
I am weak emotionally, physically
dying slowly, rolling on to my back I was cold,
I wasn't sure if it was my body
getting cold or a breeze from the crisp night air.
He did it with ease I shout with the
little bit of strength I have.
I have been yelling so much that
I had a crucial case of dry mouth,
which left me coughing and still crying,
turning my head to the right to waddle in my puddle
and I noticed the strangest thing,
a rainbow shining through the blood
and teary mix as if it had rained.
I put away the yelling for a moment,
sat straight up and thinking to myself
this couldn't be happening.

121

I peak over my shoulder to the concrete side walk
I have been lying on for what
seemed like over 24 hours.
The puddle was still there
and the rainbow was still shining out
of a puddle of blood.
If I had the strength to get my camera I would,
surely the world has never seen this
before but they should.
Now focused on this amazing phenomenon,
my tears were drying up and my pain was calmed,
looking down at my shirt the blood was gone.
I grabbed at my breast where the pain once lay,
clenching at what I thought was a stab wound,
rubbing my face searching for the wetness of tears,
suddenly it was ok,
looking back to find the puddle
which seemed like it was never there
the concrete disappears,
sitting on the floor in my bedroom
beside my bed I find myself damn near scared.
Trying to recall what just happened,
holding the phone in my right hand,
at it I stare asking myself again
what just happened here.
What did he just say to make me feel
this way what did he just do,
he told me I love her way more than
I love you!
Sitting back I rest my head against my bed
even though I am not bleeding I still feel dead.
And a loud strong voice spoke
having something to tell me,
God sent the rainbow to tell you to
get up Celeste!

Finishing my writing I throw down my pen and pad as I do most of the time I am writing through emotion. Crawling into bed I start to cry again, looking over to where he normally sleeps and wanting to feel his big chocolate body swallow me up and keep me warm. The next morning I feel like I have a midget sitting on my chest, realizing how stupid I had been, his mom knew, his brothers knew, all of his friends knew. They were all looking at me be stupid, watching him play me. I feel so deceived. Trinity even expressed how she went to dinner at Mrs. Di's house several times. I thought that Mrs. Di and I had a great relationship, but after finding this out I am looking at all of his family and friends side-ways.

His grandma calls me early that morning. "Look, I didn't know anything about that girl, I don't even know that girl, but I know you and I love you and I love those kids. Look, don't you cry, when my husband was living he cheated on me and he told me one day, that girl's pussy looks better than your face." Now I am not focusing on my hurt. For a second I am at full attention to her voice in my hear. Still crying, I gasp when she tells me what he said. "Yes, he did, so don't you cry over no man!" I am feeling a little hope when she spoils it by saying, "Mitchell loves you, don't you worry about that girl, Mitchell loves you."

"No he doesn't, Grandma, if he loved me he wouldn't hurt me."

She argues that he does and that he is just confused.

"Okay, Grandma, I will talk to you later." I don't want to be rude. I know she means well, so I just need to get off the phone with her and go back to crying and being depressed. My eyes are open but my heart, soul, and body are so heavy that I can't move. Laying there contemplating moving, "Get up, Celeste."

Rolling out of bed I call in to work sick. Love sick, so hurt I am feeling sick. I get my kids off to school and return home.

Music is what I need, India Arie's Voyage to India first and now I'm playing Brandy's Aphrodisiac,laying on the couch. Feeling as if Brandy has been a fly on the wall for the past two years I am crying my heart out, nose runny, can hardly breathe, crying like when your grandma whips you with a tree branch and calls it a switch.

Still unable to move, as I am considering making a move to the bathroom until there is a knock on the door. Being that I can't move I ignore it. Knock after knock after knock...I figure they will just go away in a minute. Finally a key turns and in walks Mitchell. I am immovable as if nothing is happening, lifeless. Walking over and sitting in front of me to my left at my computer desk he stares at me. When I look into his face it is a different Mitchell, not my Mitchell, not the Mitchell I fell in love with. He starts to speak, but my music is blasting. Staring face up at the ceiling I wipe a tear away.

"Can I talk to you?!" he yells over the music. I am still not moving, he walks over and turns the music down and returns to his seat at the computer table.

"Look, Mitchell," I start, "all I want is for you to be happy, if you're happy you can be with her. Why did you do this to me? I have told you over and over again to just go ahead and be with her, you didn't have to do this."

He responds with his head down, saying, "I have been praying for all this to come to an end. I have been talking to a pastor that works with me and I have been telling him how I want to stop playing this game. I didn't want to hurt anyone. I am sorry Celeste, I haven't cried since my dad died, now I can't stop, I am sorry."

Now standing, I ask him to leave. He stands and approaches me, asking me to forgive him. Pushing him away I scream, "Just get out!"

He grabs me and kisses me passionately. "I love you, I am sorry," he whispers, kissing me between every word. We end up naked and on the floor. He has a flow as calm and constant as an ocean wave. I exhale and loosen the tension in my gut. This is not just sex, it is love making. A different level of emotion and passion, he is inside me and I am inside him, our souls intertwine. He will not leave my side, he stays with me all day and all night for about a week. He is catering to me, taking me out, taking care of the kids.

Days go by and sex is constant, without effort, the greatest sex ever. It is like our souls are combined. Synchronized breathing patterns and orgasms...love is defined between us again.

Life goes on and so does our relationship. He says that he had finished things off with Trinity and the only reason he told me he loved her more than me was because he was mad at me for trying to set him up with us in the house together.

Friends and family think I am crazy for being so caught up. I feel stupid sometimes and I have no one I can really talk to anymore. Even though my friends never come out and actually say it, I know they have written me off as being stupid for taking all of this. I am so caught up that being caught up doesn't dawn on me until Mitchell calls one day.

"Hey baby, wassup. We need to talk."

"kay, wassup," I say very curiously.

"I think that Trinity may be pregnant."

"What! Why do you think that?"

"She has been making little comments like soon I will have you, soon you will have to be with me. She will call me and leave crazy voicemails saying she can't live without me and if I am not with her I won't be with anybody. The last time I was there I didn't see any of her usual feminine products."

"When were you there last?"

"It's been a while but I don't know. I think she is trying to wait until she can't have an abortion to tell me."

"When you ask her, what does she say?"

125

"She avoids the question. She won't even talk to me long. She will just say something crazy and hang up the phone. I wanted to call you because I am going to buy a test tomorrow, go to her house, and demand she take it or I will expose some nasty truths at her job the next day."

"Okay, Celeste," I think to myself, at least he called to let you know. "Well, I want you to call me when you are on your way, call me when you get in the house, and call me when you leave."

"Damn! Baby, what do you think I am going to do?"

"How easy do you think it is to trust you right now, Mitchell?"

"Okay, okay, I will do it."

"I sit in another state of shock again for the what, fifth or sixth time in this relationship. Now I feel like I am going in circles, losing myself. "What if she is?" I ask myself. "What will I do?"

Mitchell spends the night with me that night but it slips my mind so we didn't even talk about what the test results were. However, he is acting strange the whole night and I am wondering why. The next day my house phone starts ringing at 6 in the morning. I don't answer and I get a message. As I listen to the voicemail, Trinity is crying and explaining, "Celeste, Mitchell doesn't want you to know but I am having his baby. He doesn't want to tell you that we are going to be together and raise our child."

I look at Mitchell laying in my bed while I listen to this message. Waking him up I say, "So you know she's pregnant!"

"Yes, I didn't know how to tell you."

"So what now?" I ask as the phone rings again. I answer, hoping it's Trinity.

"Celeste!" yells Ms. Di. "Where is Mitchell?"

"He is here, let me speak to him." All of his answers to her were okay, uh huh, okay.

"Take me to my mom's house, I have to explain this to her," he insists. "Trinity has been calling her all morning but she didn't answer the phone." As he asked I drop him off at his mother's house. We ride in silence the whole way. I don't know how to respond to this and he doesn't know how to explain it to me.

CHAPTER 9.

She's His Baby Mama!

As I arrive back home, my phone rings again. I see that its Trinity. "Yes, I am having his baby, he didn't want to tell you," she says. Since it was her third attempt to call me I felt like I should answer the phone.

"Okay," I respond to her surprise. "I will help Mitchell take care of the baby."

"What do you mean? Why would you want to share him?"

"How is that sharing him? I am sorry to inform you that a baby does not keep a man, Trinity."

"So, you still want to be with him?"

"Yes," I reply. I was unsure of that answer but I would never let her know I was.

She hangs up the phone on me, very disappointed that her game to trap Mitchell doesn't work on me. Trinity arrives at Mitchell's house as his mom is dropping him off. He is on the phone with me and I hear Trinity crying and yelling in the background.

"I will call you back in a minute," he says in an irritated voice. About ten minutes later, he calls me back.

"Guess what, Celeste!"

"Wassup?"

"My brother let this girl in the house last night and she slept under my bed until I got home."

"ARE YOU SERIOUS?! That's crazy...where is she now?"

"She is in the living room laying on the floor crying."

"Where are you?"

"I am in my room folding clothes. I am not thinking about that crazy girl."

"Well, call me back later because we need to talk about all of this." As we hang up the phone, I go to the bathroom and cry. My heart is hurting. We talked about having a baby and now he is going to have a baby by her. Sitting on the toilet fully clothed with the fan on so that no one can hear me crying, I start to pray. "Lord, I need you to take this love I have for him away from me. Make me strong."

That night he calls me back. "Let's go to the park tomorrow and talk about this," he suggests. The park is one of our favorite things to do. We will just sit outside and talk for hours about whatever comes to mind.

The next day at the park the conversation is different from what I thought it would be. Yes, I was so hurt, and he sounded so sincere with every word. "So, what are you going to do?" I ask. "Do you want to be with her because of the baby? If so, I understand," I say as I drop my head in anticipation of him agreeing to be with her.

"But what if I want to be with you?"

Raising my head with a slight grin, I ask, "Do you?"

"Yes, I do."

"Are you sure?"

"Yes, you make me happy, nobody does the silly things that we do to make each other happy, like playing last tag and punch bug." We laugh together and continue to enjoy the day. He stays with me all day and all night and a week passes by. I am unusually happy. Not knowing that there wouldn't be many more laughs after that.

I call Keisha and tell her that Trinity is pregnant. She sighs and ask, "When is enough going to be enough for you?" After I get off the phone with her those words ring in my head for weeks.

Months are starting to pass and doctor's appointments are rolling around. "Mitchell, there is no reason for you to go to every doctor's appointment!"

"But I like to hear the baby's heartbeat, I like to know what's going on. I talk to you all the way there and as soon as I get out, I am not doing anything with her."

"I never said you were, but when you go to the doctor's appointments she doesn't look at it like you're going for the baby. She thinks you're going for her." This is an ongoing argument, I am constantly crying and praying every night. Some nights I cry in the bathroom while he is asleep in my bed. I have nobody to talk to. All of my friends have turned a deaf ear to me. What have I gotten myself into? Can I really deal with this? Who am I kidding? I decide no, I can't do this, so I tell him, "I can't do this anymore, Mitchell."

"Yes, you can, we can do this together," he pleads.

"Have you told her that you don't want to be with her? Does she even know we are together?"

"Yes, she knows I am not going to be with her."

"I don't believe you, I want you to call her in front of me and tell her."

"Why? That is not necessary, you know she is crazy. She may lose the baby or something. She may try to lose the baby on purpose or hurt herself."

She has him dumbfounded but I know better. She wants that baby more than anything just to keep a strong hold on him. Which means more crying nights for me, but I am all smiles all day. I am in love. "I love him right," I ask my mirror one night. "Don't I love him?" I know that I love him but that really isn't the issue. The real question is how much does he love me, that he will do all of this to me?

Memorial weekend rolls around and my cousins and I decide to take a trip to Miami and so do Mitchell and some of his friends. Mitchell is making little to no money and I have a little cash, so I loan him $500. I have no problem doing it, he is my man and I love him. Plus that is nothing compared to the $1000 cut I took off the top of my tax money for him that year just so he could get back on his feet.

We get off the plane in Miami International Airport! I step into hot groggy weather, not a drop of moisture in the air but I know I am going to have a ball. I had lost a little weight and found a magic temporary cure to stretch marks, some cream that matches my skin tone and looks great. I am feeling good. We have minor problems with our hotel but we intend to make the best of it. We all fly down on Thursday. Mitchell and I are on different flights but keep in contact with each other.

Starting Friday night, I decide I am about to make this a good weekend for me. I have been going through hell back in Alabama and I need to breath. After Meka, Erica, and I decide on a club, we also decide that our goal is to have a great time. "What happens in Miami stays in Miami!" we yell as we slip on the last essential elements of our outfits. My extra short red skirt I bought from one of the stores on the strip is looking extra sexy along with my black heels lacing up my legs and my black halter with a shoestring tie around the neck. It's MIA...we're letting it all hang out.

As we walk out of the room Mitchell and Corn are posted up across the street. I want to walk by as if I don't even know him, but of course, we stop for a moment. "DAMN!! Girl, you are looking good," says a guy walking by looking me up and down and me standing with Mitchell behind me. I am posing like the guy's eyes are a camera. Mitchell steps up beside me as if to show his presence in this situation.

"Okay, girls, I am ready to go." Meka explains. Erica and I don't object so we walk over to Washington Avenue to hit the club. We stop at the second one we find and go in. The music is pumping, we look good, and we know it. After a few drinks we are partying. We look over to where the VIP area is located and we see a couple of skinny girls on a stage dancing. At first we think they work for the club or something but then the DJ starts inviting girls to get on stage. We look at each other and are thinking the same thing at the same time, "Let's go show them how the thick girls do it!" We slap hands and make our way over to the VIP area. We get on the stage and take over. We are all thick, thighs and ass just jiggling, thick not fat. Since I had been bartending in a strip club I know just how to make it clap.

Guys are throwing money and we are shaking our money makers. We make at least fifty dollars apiece and we keep our clothes on, besides Erica showing a butt cheek or two. After the club we retire to the room. It is about 5 in the morning and we are all feeling good.

The next night we are having trouble finding a club we want to go to. I get a call from Corn, "Celeste, I can't stand going places with this dude man, he always getting drunk and acting stupid."

"Corn, slow down, wassup."

"Man, I have lost this nigga man, he drunk talking about he security with some local rappers down here."

"Okay, I will meet you and help you find him." We walk up and down the strip looking for Mitchell. He would answer the phone but is drunk and keeps on talking about how he is security. Corn gets mad and goes back to their room. Once I decide to give up and go back to my room, I spot Mitchell across the street from my hotel. I walk over to him to start fussing but he starts with the security story and I have to laugh. I lose track of the fact that I am so mad at him. He is silly drunk but surprisingly walking straight.

We walk down to the beach just to see the water at night.

But we end up doing more than that. Sitting in the sand side by side, I climb of top of him and the waves define our motion after that. He rolls on top of me, looking at the dark Miami night sky the stars are aligned and everything is right. The sound of the ocean seems to get louder and louder as we reach orgasm at the same time. We lay beside each other in the sand listening to the waves and feeling as one with the ocean, not thinking about the fact that we didn't use any protection.

After about thirty minutes he falls asleep and I am ready to go back to my room. I shake him but he is so drunk he can hardly move. I am tipsy myself but now I have to sober up quickly to get him back to the hotel. Finally I get him up, his 240 pound chocolate body depending on me to walk. He stays at my room that night because he is too drunk to make it back to his room. While he is asleep I go through his phone and see that he had been calling Trinity since we arrived in MIA. But I don't argue about it – I just make a mental note of it.

Monday comes and it's time to go back home. I am missing my babies but not my issues back home. When we get back, Mitchell and I are in agreement that we can work this thing out. About three weeks pass by and one Friday we decide to go out to this club that recently opened up downtown. It is a nice night – not too hot, not too cold. We go to the club, have a good time, and start back to the house. I give him head all the way to my house and he is loving it. The anticipation is so high for both of us that by the time we get home, all he really has to do is lay in it and that he does. Like no other man has. We agree that the sex between us is not normal. It is on the highest level of sex. We are completely bound by emotions.

The next morning everything is cool until I get a knock at my door. For some reason, for the past two days I have been feeling unusually sick in the mornings but I think nothing of it. I get up to answer the door but take a detour to the bathroom. I yell to Mitchell to open the door and close the bathroom door behind me. I sit down on the toilet but I don't have to do number 2. I get on my knees and start to throw up. I keep a pregnancy test under my bathroom cabinet. I already have two children; I am a highly fertile person. If you look at me the wrong way I might get pregnant. As I reach for the test I hear people talking outside but I ignore it and continue on to take the test.

Meanwhile outside, "Trinity! What are you doing here?!" yells Mitchell.

"No, what are you doing here, Mitchell? You said you were going to be with me! You said you wanted to be a family!"

"Come on, come on," I whisper as I pace the bathroom floor. "Positive. AAAHHH!!!" I scream.

Mitchell and Trinity hear this from the bottom of the steps outside the house. Mitchell leaves Trinity in the middle of her sentence to come to my rescue. Banging on the bathroom door, he shouts, "Celeste!! Open the door! What's wrong?!"

I open the door and Trinity walks up behind him. I am too devastated about the test results to even think about why the hell she is at my house. "Look," I say as I hold up the test showing a pink plus sign for positive. Mitchell and Trinity's mouths drop wide open. She is about 5 months pregnant at this point and this is the first time I saw her pregnant since I found out.

"You did this on purpose, bitch!" Trinity shouts and hurries out of the front door. I am on my way to go outside and bust her in the face but Mitchell stops me.

"Oh, hell, no, she didn't come to my house. I am about to beat this bitch ass."

"Let me handle it. Let me handle it," he says. He goes outside and I am grabbing for any type of clothing to put on and cussing at the same time.

"No, this bitch didn't come to my house and my kids are

here too. She has lost her damn mind. I will beat her pregnant ass all the way back to her car."

I go outside to see what's going on and they are standing at the bottom of my steps talking. She is acting as if she is about to leave but when she sees me she comes back. Now I am at the bottom of the steps.

"Celeste, go back in the house."

"No, you pregnant and you coming to my house while my kids are here, what the hell is wrong with you? I could beat your ass right now and it would not even matter to me. I could drag you all up and down these steps and not think a thing about it."

"Whatever...if you think I am crazy I will show you," she says, rolling her eyes.

"But it's not about you, it's about Mitchell," I continue.

"Are you going to be with her, Mitchell?!" she shouts.

I look at Mitchell anticipating an answer and he doesn't say anything.

"Tell her, Mitchell, tell her, are you going to be with me?"

"Look, Trinity, just leave," is all he says. I look at him in awe. All of us are in a state of shock and frustration. Him from the news we just got, me from her being at my house and the news we just got, her from the news and the fact that he is over my house.

"After everything we discussed this week, you can't tell her yes, you're going to be with me?" I ask.

"Are you going to be with her, Mitchell?!" Trinity shouts again. "I don't have time for this," she says and walks back to her car.

By this time I am boiling over. "So why didn't you tell her, Mitchell? Why couldn't you just say yes?"

"Look, I am here with you. I was telling her to leave because I wanted to be here with you and you are tripping, plus how the hell did you get pregnant?"

135

"I hate you! Get your stuff. I want you out of my house!" I shout, stomping up the steps.

Well, we rode together to the club so I have to drive him back home. We argue all the way there...the same argument we have had for the past three years.

"Why can't you just tell her?"

"What would it change, Celeste?"

"What do you mean what would it change? Then I will know that you really don't want to be with her."

When we pull up to his house, Trinity is pulling up behind us. She gets out of the car and knocks on his window for him to get out of the car. He gets out of the car and we are arguing into the house. She is just following behind us into the house.

"Tell her, why can't you just tell her? You're not going to mess up my life, Celeste!"

Huh? Just the other day he wanted to be with me and not her. Now cuz she's in our presence the story changes.

CHAPTER 10.

Add a Litttle Salt to the Drama

This is the point when I realize I can't take it anymore. I leave there and cry until my body's tear factory shuts down. I drive around the city for hours, crying and praying as always. "Lord, take this love I have for him away from me. Now I am pregnant, she is pregnant, what the hell happened here? Where did it all go wrong?" I question myself over and over again.

He calls me later that night. "Oh my God. Baby. you are pregnant."

"Yes, I know that dumbass but I am not having it," I say in a hateful voice.

"Why? You are not killing my baby so what is your plan?"

"What do you mean what is my plan? Go into your savings and let's head to the clinic, nigga." I hate him but I want my baby. It is something he and I had always talked about. I am crying my heart out but saying, "I am not having this baby."

"Celeste, please," he begs. "If you don't want it then let me have it."

"NO! So you can have my baby being taken care of by her, hell no!"

"Well, let's be together." He tries to give me every reason

why I should keep the baby but I refuse to go through the drama with Trinity forever as being one of his baby mamas. He offers to do whatever I want. He says he will tell her he didn't want her, he would stop talking to her, and he would not take care of her baby, but me trying to be a good person, I say, "No, Mitchell, that's your baby, you should take care of it."

That next Monday we end up at the clinic. Mitchell cries harder than I do and I am disgusted with him. It takes about an hour and a half and it is done. I regret it, I really want him and my baby, but it doesn't feel right.

Months are passing fast and Trinity is getting bigger. He is saying the same things and we are having the same arguments but I am dating other people now. I am still working at the bar and I am meeting guys there. The regulars I am never attracted to because I know what they want, but the guys who stop by every now and then are worth taking a chance on. I am often depressed.

Working at the bar relieves my tension because I feel like it is the only place in the world that has more drama than me. Bopping my head to the beat and making drinks for a crowd of people I have my back turned and I hear a guy shout, "I'll have whatever she's making!"

I turn and look at one of the other bartenders and she looks at me. "I think this one's yours!" she shouts over the music. The strip club is small enough to just fit 100-150 people, if that. There are two stages. The girls dance on the big stage, which is in the front, and the small stage, which is at the back. The stages are lined with lights and mirrors and, of course, a silver pole right down the middle. The dancers are cool, but not very trustworthy.

They are about their money and that is understood; as bartenders, so are we. The bar area is a small rectangular-shaped area only big enough for two people to work comfortably.

The customers are always flirting and I am never amused by it. Plus, I am a mad black woman at this point anyway. I walk back over to the bar with an attitude, screw facing him. He is short, about 5'10, very dark and smooth skinned. He has long flowing neat dreads. When I was in college I had a thing for men with dreads, until I found that the dreads are a hassle when they slap you in the face during sex.

"Malachi," he introduces himself. He is cute, but I don't care...I have had enough of men and their charm.

"What can I get for you?"

"Damn, baby, it can't be that bad. Just smile for me, that's all I need."

"What do you want nigga?" I say harshly to let him know his flirting is not working. We have to be like that behind the bar because the strip club is a very conniving place. No one in the club can be trusted.

Pulling out a $50 he says, "Honestly, I just want to see you smile."

I still am not amused. Normally in bartending, money talks, but I am just not in the mood for another no good man. Without entertaining the $50, I ask another customer for his drink order. "Okay, Okay, miss, just get me a Grey Goose and pineapple." I fix the drink and give it to him. He already knows the price because he had been there before.

There is a mirror stretched across the wall behind the bar. As I am getting his change from the cash register I notice that he drops the $50 in my tip jar and walks away from the bar to have a seat at a table.

The night goes on and ends as usual. As I am cleaning the bar he approaches me again. "Excuse me, miss, just talk to me a second."

"What is it? You can't possibly want to talk to me that bad."

"Why do you say that? Let me take you out sometime."

139

"Sorry, I am not interested."

"Well, here is my card. Call me sometime, it can't hurt just to converse a little."

I take the card and slip it into my back pocket.

Mitchell and I are still having sex constantly. We have sex as much as we can. We still go out for lunch; we never officially say it is over. He begs me to let go of the past and live on together happy but I am unhappy, my self esteem is low. I feel he cheated on me because I am fat, because of the kids, because I'm not good enough. I question him frequently but he says, "I don't know why I did it. I love the kids, I don't think you are fat, but I know I want to be with you now."

The doctor's appointments with Trinity seem like they are days apart and I hate him, her, and myself. I start eating to comfort myself, then I take a laxative every other day and I am never satisfied with myself. I have to do something...I have to make a move. I go days without talking to him and he calls, leaving begging messages. I sit and cry as I listen to everyone of them.

In the laundry one day out comes this card from that guy at the bar that night. After a few minutes of thinking I decide to call him, hey, why not. We talk for hours, asking questions about each other. I ask him how he got his name because it is not very common. He explains that it is in the Bible, which I know. I am just trying to keep the conversation going. I have always thought that Malachi is a peculiar name, but now that I have taken the time out to call him I think it is sexy. We hit it off great. I start to date him on a regular basis which means less and less time thinking about Mitchell. Malachi and I go out to dinner on nights that I'm not working at the club. I don't allow him around my kids and I'm not ready to have sex with anyone but Mitchell.

Mitchell and I are still having sex and I don't tell him about Malachi. He always asks, "What are you doing tonight since

140

you are off?"

"I don't know...a little bit of this and a little bit of that."

"What the hell does that mean?"

"I don't know. Maybe you should ask your baby mama, ha ha ha," I laugh as I rush him to get off the phone. He hates for me to call her his baby mama, and because of the fact that he is still begging me to be with him despite everything that is going on he is not amused. I am starting to feel like I am getting over him a little. But for some reason I feel safe having sex with him even though now I know for sure that he is still having sex with her.

One night about 10 p.m. Malachi calls. "Wassup Lesty!" He calls me Lesty when he wants to see me and I love it.

"Nothing, watching some TV and very close to going to bed."

"I know it's late but can I come over?"

I have an unexpected night off and the kids are in bed, so I agree. "I am letting you know now that I know it's about 10 p.m. You can come over but I do not want to have sex."

"Who said anything about having sex? Girl you are tripping, I just want to see you."

"That's cool, but I don't want any miscommunications. It's a known fact that when guys want to come over late at night they don't want to watch TV."

"See you been messing with those young boys." Malachi is about three years older than me, but he doesn't know who he was talking to because I have always been with older men. DJ is like 3 years older than me, Damari is 5 years older than me, and Mitchell is 2 years older than me. He must think I am stupid. Having a child at a young age will make you grow up quick.

"Okay, Malachi, come over," I say with regret, because I am not convinced that he is being truthful. I make sure I stay fully dressed to let him know I am not playing. We watch a movie

141

and I am getting sleepy. I fall asleep laying across his lap as he is running his fingers through my hair, which is a no-no. It is relaxing and I am tired, plus he has already screamed about how he is not going to try anything.

After being asleep a few minutes I notice a rub on my thigh, then between my legs so I jump up. "I told you that I was not going there with you."

"It's cool. I was just rubbing you down making you feel relaxed."

"Well, thank you, but it's getting late. I think it's time for you to go." I get up, pull him up, and walk him to the door. As we approach the door he starts to kiss me. It has been so long since I kissed anyone but Mitchell that I feel disgusting at first. Soon I am giving in and we end up in my bed. Laying on my back as he pulls off my pants, I am coming into the realization of how much a hold Mitchell really has on me. I am looking up at the ceiling again. For some reason I always use the ceiling as my focal point, but I am feeling so emotional, all I can think about is Mitchell. I feel like I am cheating on him or something. As Malachi goes down on me he is there all of three minutes when I scream, "Stop! You gotta go, I can't do this!"

I jump up out of the bed and grab my pants. Beginning to dress myself I am almost in tears and asking him to leave.

"Okay, okay, I will leave. It's cool, I am sorry." As I lock the door behind him I sigh and lay across my bed wishing that I could rewind time and make a different decision. A decision to leave Mitchell's ass alone a long time ago, a decision to move to Maryland after school, and at this moment a decision to get Mitchell out of my system.

The next morning I am over it. I am glad that I didn't have intercourse with him, I just don't want anyone but Mitchell. So two days later Mitchell comes over and we have sex again. I go to his job and we have sex in his office. It is like we can't resist each other. Over a period of thirty days the sex starts to feel different. I am starting to feel some itching and some pain. I think maybe it is an allergic reaction to condoms because we are using them on and off. It gets to the point where my vagina is hurting not just during sex, but during baths and when I wipe myself after using the bathroom.

I am getting concerned so I decide to go and get it checked out. The doctor confirms that I have contracted Herpes Simplex 1. He explains how common Herpes is and the statistics on people who have it, which were very high, but still not me. When the doctor tells me this I am in shock. I don't know whether to run out of the office or break down in tears. I am angry with Mitchell for having sex with Trinity and me at the same time. I blame her for giving it to me because I haven't had sex with anyone but Mitchell. I begin asking the doctor lots of questions; questions about how you get it and how I prevent myself from giving it to somebody. The doctor explains that "Herpes Simplex 1 is simply a cold sore. I am sure you have family members who get cold sores on their lips every now and then. This is the exact same thing except you have it on your vagina."

"So what does that mean? Does that mean that I got it through oral sex?"

"It could mean that you got it through oral sex or from someone else who had Herpes Simplex 1 in their pubic area."

This means that there is a chance that I got it from Malachi, but he was only down there for no longer than 3 minutes and he didn't have any sores on his mouth. This could also mean that I could have gotten it from Trinity or Mitchell. After leaving the doctor's office I immediately call Mitchell and tell him the bad news. Because he doesn't really have a job, he has no insurance and has to go to urgent care. He comes up positive. He also tells Trinity and she comes up positive.

This circle of confusion has become more than any of us

can handle. Trinity doesn't even get as upset as I thought. Normally she is blowing up my phone or popping up at my house if she feels that Mitchell is with me, but after finding out that there is a possibility that I could have given her an STD she doesn't even try to contact me. I find that very strange. I confess to Mitchell my rendezvous with Malachi and she confesses hers with some guy about two months before but Mitchell blames me. Because it is Simplex 1 he is convinced that it is my fault because of the oral sex.

"See what you did! You didn't even know this dude and you just letting him go down on you, what the hell is wrong with you? Now you have given this shit to me and Trinity!"

"How are you just going to blame this on me? She had sex with another dude and the doctor said that you can get Simplex 1 from someone else who has Simplex 1."

"But she had sex with that dude a long time ago."

"You know what, Mitchell, the truth of the matter is I didn't give it to her, YOU DID!" Hanging up the phone on him feels so good.

Now there is only one last person to call and that is Malachi. "Hi, Malachi." My voice sounds a little frantic because I just hung up the phone with Mitchell.

"Wassup babe?" he asks in a concerned tone.

"I have a question for you, do you get cold sores on your mouth?"

"Every now and then, but I haven't had one in like a year. Why, wassup?"

I give him the entire story about Trinity and Mitchell and he is quiet.

"I am sorry you had to go through that, if you like I will go get tested."

"The thing about herpes is you can't get tested until you have an outbreak. If you get your blood tested it will let you know you have it but it doesn't let you know if it appears on

144

your mouth or your pubic area."

"Well I will get tested, anyway, just for you." Malachi is sweet, but he is not my type. He is too short and smokes cigarettes. A guy that smokes cigarettes is a major turn off for me.

After getting off the phone with him I just sit alone thinking, "How will I live now?" Everyone usually overlooks having cold sores on your mouth, but when people say they have herpes some people freak out or think they are nasty. I find myself crying and praying once again. This seems to be the story of my life. "Why me, I am a good girl, I am not promiscuous, I don't have sex with just anybody!" I yell out to God.

The next day I start using the cream and taking the pills but I am depressed. I get a call from Malachi saying that his test is positive. He is sure that he does get cold sores from time to time but he says he didn't have one when he went down on me and somehow I believe him. Mitchell doesn't, he believes Trinity and blames me. At this point I am saying whatever and just trying to deal with myself.

A week goes by and I am avoiding Mitchell. Even though he is upset with me he is still leaving me messages saying he wants to be with me. I am just devastated. Now I am a single parent with two children by two different daddies and I have a recurring STD. Who the hell will want me now?

Life can't stop because of that so I continue working and hiding how I am really feeling with a smile. Teaching is rewarding for me. My troubles cannot compare to the trouble that some of these kids are dealing with and while I am teaching it is all about them.

One day, Mitchell calls me and I decide to answer. It has been about two weeks since we found out about the STD or had a real conversation. We have the ability to click no matter what. We can only be mad at each other for a short while. We have the kind of love for each other that will always prevail and it is because of our friendship. Trinity is jealous of the friendship between me and Mitchell because we always end up talking things out no matter how bad he hurts me or how many times she pops up. My relationship with his family is just as tight. I continue to eat dinners at Mrs. Di's and she and I are repairing our relationship.

During this phone conversation he asks if he can come over that night so I agree. The sexual escapades begin again. The sex between us is unbelievable. The anticipation itself is enough to make a movie out of. The energy flows like a running faucet and when it is time to go down, anything goes. We continue with this sexual addiction we have to each other. Hey, we both had the STD, so we feel more comfortable having sex with each other.

I am enjoying the sex but my conscience is beating me up. Trinity is still having his baby and I cannot handle that emotionally. I feel so in love with him. How can this be if it is not meant to be?

CHAPTER 11.

Make a Move Girl!

I start to evaluate my situation. My job situation is not something I see myself doing for the rest of my life. Teaching is cool, but the school system is a big front and has no real values. I am hell emotionally and now hell physically because I am eating for comfort plus I have been diagnosed with an STD. I have what I call a "mirror talk," staring in the mirror, saying to myself, "Celeste, what are you doing? Why are you hurting yourself for this man?" These conversations end in tears because there are no answers. He has a baby by a woman he told me was nobody. I have been through many of life's adversities and I am considered a statistic in the eyes of America and I beat that. They didn't think I could survive high school because I was rebellious. They didn't think I would make it to college let alone graduate with a Bachelor of Science in Computer Science. I have seen my mom hurt trying to accept a man's wrongdoings, so after all of this why can't I let this man go? He has been in my life so long that I have forgotten what it is like not being with him. What would I do without him?

He is still coming to see me and we are still having sex but I am feeling lonely. I feel that all of my friends and family have come to the consensus that I am stupid. I can't cry on their shoulders anymore because they have given me so many warnings about ending up in this big mess.

After weeks of crying, mirror talks, and constant evaluation of my situation I wake up about 3 a.m. one morning and decide I have to get out of here. I have to move. It is like an epiphany. There is no process that is going to make this just go away or make me just get over it. I have to shake myself and JUST DO IT! I have no money to move, no idea how I am going to move, but I consult my guide, who I have been praying to so hard for answers all my life. I am intimidated by starting over and afraid of being without a man I have spent almost every day with for the last three years.

I use my tears to focus. Every time he has to go to the doctor with her or I feel like he is lying to me motivates me to get out faster. I call friends I know from college who live in other states. I go down the list of names in my phone and start pushing resumes across the Internet left and right.

There is one friend who comes through and his name is Trevor. He lives in Northern Virginia and works for one of the major delivery companies at the time. He pressures his supervisor to interview me and everything is set. I interview with the supervisor over the phone and it turns into a three-hour-long flirtatious conversation. I am asked to come to Virginia and have an in-person interview with the head manager. I get the job but there are other steps that need to be taken before I can start which can take about a month. However, I know that I can't stay here anymore. A job lead is better than nothing. I pray, pack, and cry for a month.

I call my mom, who is familiar with the ins and outs of my situation. "Come home, baby," she says in a subtle, compassionate voice. If I could just lay on her lap and cry for a moment, I would.

I tell Mitchell that I am leaving and he begs me to stay.

"Please don't go, Celeste, we can do this. We can work it out."

"How, if you're not even willing to tell her you are with me? I can't spend my life tip-toeing around another woman."

I pack up everything I have. I throw away mostly everything. I really don't want anything he touched. I have no idea how I am moving but I know that I am going to my mama's house. Every day I just start to hate to live there. Everything reminds me of him. He starts pushing me away, he won't see me or really talk to me. Trinity feels like she has won a prize because he tells her that I had an abortion and that I would be moving soon.

Mitchell and I still talk but for some reason he never lets me come over. I ask him to keep my computer because I don't want to put it in storage and he agrees. I tell him I will drop it off but he insists on coming over to get it.

It is time for Trinity's baby shower. It is Saturday and I have been begging to see him all week but he always has an excuse. I want to spend some time with him before I leave. This is the worst night of my life. I am sad all day because of the baby shower. The thought of him over there with her laughing and joking as if they would be together forever is sickening.

The baby shower is two nights before it is was time for me to be officially moved out of the state of Alabama. I ask him to spend some time with him that night after the baby shower. "Well, Trinity has to bring the gifts and everything over here so after she leaves you can come over and spend the night."

"It's already 8. If she comes over any later than that she will want to spend the night."

"No, I will kick her out, don't worry about that I will kick her out."

We talk on the phone up until the time she arrives. "Okay, Mitchell, I will give her 10 minutes and I am on my way."

"Don't come over here acting crazy, Celeste."

"It only takes 5 minutes to get some gifts out of a car, Mitchell."

We hang up the phone and I lay down and fall asleep. When I wake up it is about 1 a.m. I call his cell phone several times and he never answers. So I get up and go over there. Her car is there so I knock on the door. I ring the doorbell...nobody answers. I call him several times. I am getting angrier by the second so I begin to throw pebbles at his window. He looks out of the blinds. "Come outside! What are you looking out of the blinds for?"

Then I remember that I have a key to his car, so I get in the car and start blowing the horn. I would have driven it around the block but he didn't have any gas. I am damn near laying on the horn and getting more mad by the second. Soon, I see blue and white lights shining into the complex. It's the police. As soon as the police pull up he runs out of the house.

"Ma'am, do you live here?" the police ask.

"No, she doesn't," Mitchell answers for me.

"How long have y'all been together?"

"Three years, sir," I reply.

"Is it over?"

"No," I answer, but Mitchell answers "Yes" about a half of a second before me.

"So it's over!" I shout at him. "Is it over, Mitchell?"

"Can you tell her to give me my key to my car back?"

"This is my key!"

"Please, officer, can you tell her to give me my key back?"

"Ma'am, please give him his key back."

"He can go get it," and I throw the key across the parking lot. I look up and Trinity is standing on his fenced-in balcony looking down at us. "What the hell you looking at?" I yell. She doesn't reply. "Well, let me get my computer, officer, he has my computer in his house."

"Sir, can she get her computer? I will escort her in."

150

"Go ahead, officer."

When I walk into the house I almost break down and cry. It is like walking into a house I have never been in before. I walk in to find that she has moved in with him. Her picture is over the fireplace. The baby room is set up with blue and green, a crib to match a short chest of drawers with a changing table on top, and a TV attached to the wall in an upper corner of the room like a hospital. Her clothes are there, her shoes are there, she has even changed all the colors of the bathroom and everything.

ANGRY, HURT, every emotion you can name I am feeling. The officer helps me take my computer downstairs. I stare at Mitchell with anger the entire time I am in the house. Once again, here I am, crying, driving, and praying, "Lord, please take away this love that I have for him."

The next night I let my emotions get the best of me. It is my last night in town and my apartment is empty. I am going to stay the night with my son's aunt and leave the next morning. A couple of weeks before the baby shower I put a gun on layaway. I felt like I wanted protection, not from Trinity, but I am a single mother alone in a house with just my kids. If someone tries to hurt us I would have no defense.

I go to pick up my gun about 4 p.m. that day. I go back to my apartment to put the finishing touches on cleaning. But I have this new gun and these new hollow-tip bullets. I want to shoot. I had taken a handgun safety course so I am familiar with guns. I load one bullet and shoot off my back balcony into the woods. It feels good...it feels real good.

After leaving the apartment for the last time, all of these thoughts start coming to my head. I hate Mitchell at this point and I hate Trinity for being so dumb. She could have Mitchell, but he hurt me very badly and I want to make him hurt. So I decide to ride over to his house. Emotions are building as I turn into the apartment complex. "I am about to kill this

151

nigga and if Trinity gets in the way she is dead too," I say to myself.

I put on any gangster CD in the car just to keep my mind hyped. I park where he cannot see my car and I walk up to the door with my gun. Mitchell owns a gun too and I know that so at this point I am prepared to die. I feel like I have no meaning without him and now that he has showed me how much meaning I don't have to him, I want to show my appreciation.

I knock on the door and ask him to come outside. He disagrees and I knock on the door again. I chirp him on the Nextel, "Come outside, Mitchell."

"For what, what do I need to come out for?"

"It's only gonna take a second. I just need to talk to you for a minute." I have no conscience right now. My mind is not talking to me like it usually is besides the bad thoughts. "This nigga is going to move her in after everything I did for him. Gave him $1,000 just to help him out and never asked him to pay me back, gave this nigga $500 to go to Miami, wasted three years of my life catering to this nigga and he repays me like this. Hell no, he has to die to make it right." Sense is not making sense to me. I want to hurt him like he hurt me. I want him to feel the pain that I felt when he stabbed me in my heart.

My attempt to get him to come outside does not work. Crying, I sit down on the porch in front of the door. I cock the gun and pointed at the door. I figure if he doesn't want to open the door I will just start shooting through it. As my finger is reaching for the trigger, my cell phone rings, it is one of my best friends, Jeremy. I met him when I moved to the city but I haven't talked to him in a while. We were very cool, I know that this call had to come straight from God, since I had gotten so involved with the drama between me and Mitchell,

Jeremy was one of the friends I had pushed aside. The call came as a total surprise, I hadn't spoken to him in months and he begins the conversation by asking,

"What are you doing?"

"I am about to kill Mitchell," I reply.

"Where are you? I am coming to get you!"

"No, don't come and get me, I am prepared to die. He has killed me anyway. My heart is ripped in two, I can't let it go. Why am I the only one hurt? I did whatever he wanted me too. I put up with this bitch harassing me for two years straight. Somebody has to get hurt besides me."

"Look, Celeste, this is not what you want to do. Think about your children, you are a very pretty girl, you're intelligent, you don't need him. He doesn't make you, you make you."

Little did I know that Jeremy had hopped in the car and made it to Mitchell's place in no time. As he parks his truck, crying my eyes out, I mumble, "I have to, I have to do it." I remove the pressure from my phone to my ear and let the phone fall. As I raise the gun and point towards the door once more, I feel a warm hand cover mine and a voice says, "It's not worth it, baby. It's not worth it."

I release the gun into Jeremy's hands. He puts the safety on and helps me up and I fall to pieces on his shoulders. My legs get weak and he has to hold me up. I make it to my son's aunt's house that night. I cry myself to sleep. When I wake up the next morning, I send a text message to Trinity.

"We had made this a game, but we are the ones that got played. I am walking away from this situation not losing to you, but setting myself free. This is the greatest decision I have ever made in my life. But I wish you luck with your new baby."

Getting on the highway all I can hear in my head is the chorus of that Nas song. It's on his God Son album, track 14:

153

If heaven was a mile a way,
would I pack up my bags
and leave this world behind,
If heaven was a mile away,
or save it all for you,
if heaven was a mile a way,
would I fill the tank up with gas
and be out the front door in a flash,
before reconsidering this hell with you,
it ain't you it's the things you do
that are tearing my heart in two.
I could have failed with you,
to hell with you.

Riding down the highway that day I don't know what to expect. This road might not lead to heaven but anywhere is better than here.

I don't know if this road leads to heaven but anywhere is better than here. As I exit the city limits on 85N the sun is shining bright, but this beautiful morning appears to be cloudy and dark through my teary eyes. I predict that my sobbing will last the entire road to emancipation, but suddenly I am interrupted by a phone call. A deep voice on the other end tears into the inner chambers of my heart yet again.

Mitchell mumbles, "I...I'm sorry, baby, can we talk........"

[1]"Life is about who makes it, not about who makes it the fastest."

To be continued...................

---

1 [Kanye West, Paul Wall, GLC & T.I. - "Drive Slow (Remix)"]

CHAPTER 12.

Encouraging Words

This chapter includes one last excerpt from Celeste's note-book. When you think no one else can feel your pain, you can use this poem as a reflection from the past you are escaping and a forecast for the new beginning you are creating. This chapter is included to let others know that you are not alone in your experiences, "ALL WOMEN ARE STUPID SOMETIMES."

Understand that the people around you care for you so much that they don't want to see you hurt; however, they don't realize how much you really need them. Women every-where should open their eyes to see that you are not stupid for loving with all of your heart. One mans "trash" is another mans treasure. Doing what you feel is right for your relation-ship does not make you stupid.

Feel My Pain, Hear My Cry, See Me Rise

When the sun rises I rise with it.
Thanking the Lord for lifting my eyes
I promise him today I won't cry.

I won't bow to drama and pain,
I will not let this day be in vain.
I have survived many days of rain.
Today, I will do something new,
guide someone through,
do what I want to do.
I will be me on this day,
starting over,
looking for me,
finding me,
and embracing a new me.
Only to wake up tomorrow and do it all over again.
God is my first love and my best friend.
A new beginning here to stay,
this is my New Day.
Suddenly the new day began to get gray.
I thought I had my life under control until "love"
showed it's face.
Dangerously in love is the name
that Beyonce would use,
I call it blindfolded and
forced to walk a plank of emotional abuse,
only to get to the end and
jump into an ocean of tears.
Then he threw salt to burn in the wound of my fear.
Cuts so deep my soul is bruised.
So I love him,
some call me crazy, stupid,
and even confused.
The thing is I am starting to believe
in these words they use.
Staring at myself in the mirror screaming
BUT I LOVE HIM,

every day.
If not then why can't I walk away,
staring into a wet face of disappointment and hurt.
Feeling like I am not good enough,
wondering are all relationships this rough.
Enduring this labor of love,
looking for the outcome to be a changed man
ready to enter into a marital relationship,
baby jus let me know.
Let me know what you want this result to be,
will it be her or will it be me?
What will I do if he doesn't choose me?
If I leave now what will be the point of all
these years I've served,
now wasted.
I keep trying to walk away and
then I'm running back,
how can I live? without his touch, without us,
without his....WHAT?
How would I live without his what?
I ask myself.
His womanizing, his lies, his sexual cravings
for another woman, WHAT?
Enlightenment and evaluation start
to bring about self realization
and I am questioning myself
on why the hell am I being so patient.
This is the last time this mirror shows me
the weaker side of a strong woman.
This image had been distorted too long,
been spending too many nights crying
wondering what I am doing wrong.
This man is not my power,

he is not my life,
I CAN live,
I CAN see the world through a new pair of eyes.
Time to break free,

Feel My Pain, Hear My Cry, See Me Rise.

www.ingramcontent.com/pod-product-compliance
Lightning Source LLC
Chambersburg PA
CBHW060116260626
47160CB00005B/1908